D0506839

Violet loves to study and keep learning new things. She likes classical music and dreams of becoming a famous violinist!

Donella would eat pizza even for breakfast. Give her a screwdriver and she'll fix any engine!

Here's the ancient and very prestigious MOUSEFORD ACADEMY, where the Thea Sisters go to school and... have fun!

CALGARY PUBLIC LIBRARY

SEP   2018

Thea Stilton

PAPERCUTZ™

Thea Stilton

GRAPHIC NOVELS AVAILABLE FROM PAPERCUTZ

ALSO AVAILABLE WHEREVER E-BOOKS ARE SOLD!

#1
"The Secret
of Whale Island"

#2
"Revenge of
the Lizard Club"

#3
"The Treasure of
the Viking Ship"

#4
"Catching the
Giant Wave"

#5
"The Secret of the
Waterfall in the Woods"

#6
"The Thea Sisters and
the Mystery at Sea"

#7
"A Song for the
Thea Sisters"

#8
"The Thea Sisters and the
Secret Treasure Hunt"

THEA STILTON graphic novels are available for $9.99 each only in hardcover. Also available from book and e-book e-retailers. You can also order online from papercutz.com or call 1-800-886-1223 Monday through Friday, 9 – 5 EST, MC-Visa, and Amex accepted. To order by mail please add $4.00 for postage and handling for first book ordered, $1.00 for each additional book, and make check payable to NBM Publishing. Send to: Papercutz, 160 Broadway, Suite 700, East Wing, New York, NY 10038.

papercutz.com

Thea Stilton

THE SECRET OF WHALE ISLAND

By Thea Stilton

PAPERCUTZ™

THE SECRET OF WHALE ISLAND
© EDIZIONI PIEMME 2008 S.p.A.
Corso Como 15, 20145,
Milan, Italy
Geronimo Stilton and Thea Stilton names, characters and related indicia are copyright,
trademark and exclusive license of Atlantyca S.p.A.
All rights reserved.
The moral right of the author has been asserted.

Text by Thea Stilton
Editorial coordination by Lorenza Bernardi and Patrizia Puricelli
With the collaboration of Serena Bellani
Artistic Coordination by Flavio Ferron
With the assistance of Tommaso Valsechi
Editing by Katja Centomo and Francesco Artibani
Editing Coordination and Artwork Supervision by Stefania Bitta and Maryam Funicelli
Script Supervision by Francesco Artibani
Script by Francesco Artibani and Caterina Mognato
Design by Giada Perissinotto
Color by Giulia Basile and Ketty Formaggio
Art by Cristina Giorgilli and Raffaella Seccia
With the assistance of Michela Battaglin and Marta Lorini
Cover by Giada Perissinotto (design), Raffaella Seccia (art), and Giulia Basile (color)

Based on an original idea by Elisabetta Dami.
© 2013 – for this work in English language by Papercutz.
Original title: "Il Secreto Dell'Isola Delle Balene"
Translation by: Nanette McGuinness
www.geronimostilton.com

Stilton is the name of a famous English cheese. It is a registered trademark of the
Stilton Cheese Makers' Association. For more information go to www.stiltoncheese.com

No part of this book may be stored, reproduced or transmitted in any form or by any means,
electronic or mechanical, including photocopying, recording, or by any information storage
and retrieval system, without written permission from the copyright holder.
FOR INFORMATION PLEASE ADDRESS ATLANTYCA S.p.A.
Via Leopardi 8 20123 Milan Italy tel. 0039 02 43001025 – fax 0039 02 43001020
Foreign Rights @ Atlantyca.it - www.atlantyca.com

Papercutz books may be purchased for business or promotional use. For information on bulk purchases
please contact Macmillan Corporate and Premium Sales Department at (800) 221-7945 x5442.

Lettering and Production -- Ortho
Production Coordinator -- Beth Scorzato
Associate Editor – Michael Petranek
Jim Salicrup
Editor-in-Chief

ISBN: 978-1-59707-403-2

Printed in China.
March 2018

Distributed by Macmillan
Fifth Papercutz Printing

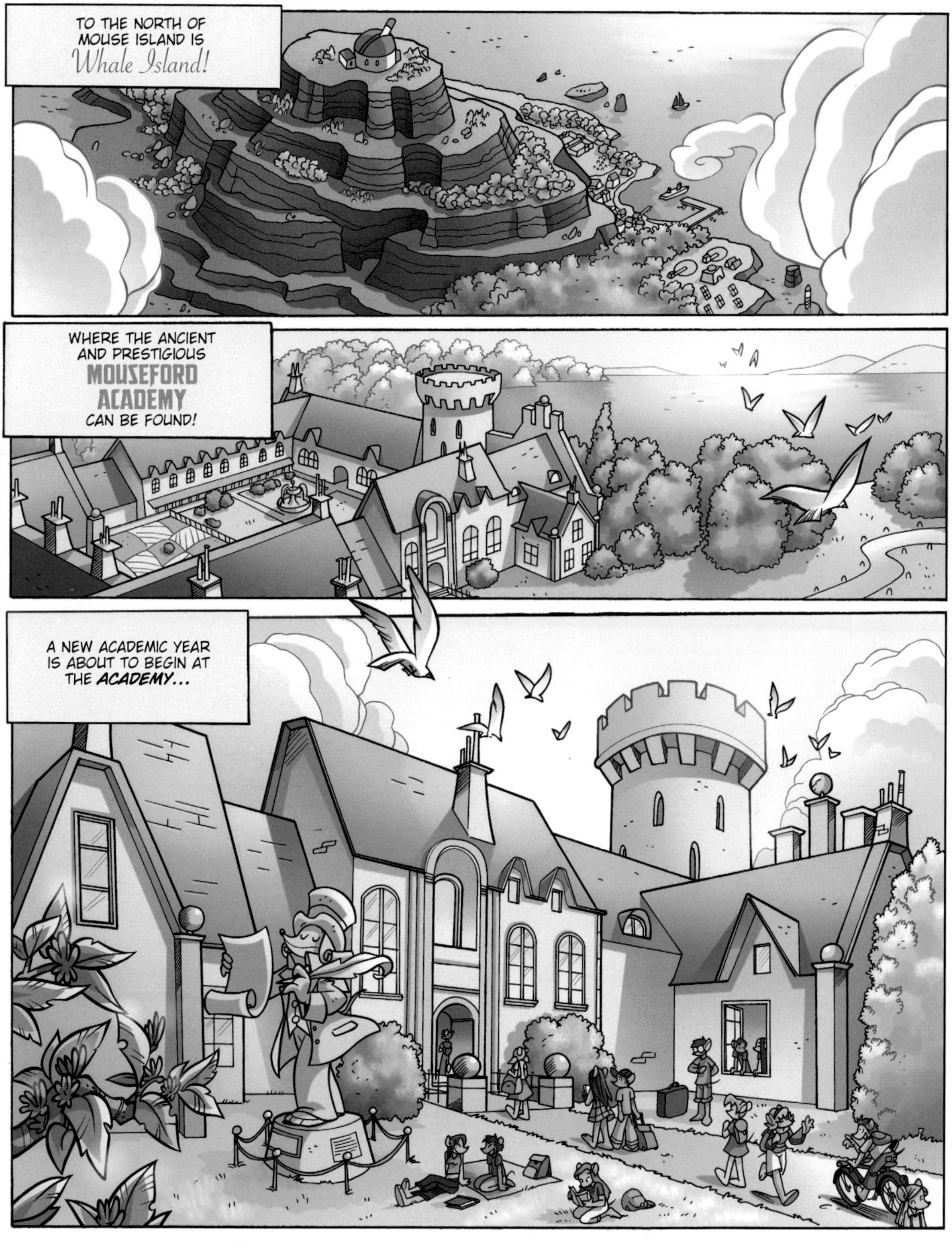
TO THE NORTH OF MOUSE ISLAND IS *Whale Island!*
WHERE THE ANCIENT AND PRESTIGIOUS **MOUSEFORD ACADEMY** CAN BE FOUND!
A NEW ACADEMIC YEAR IS ABOUT TO BEGIN AT THE ***ACADEMY...***

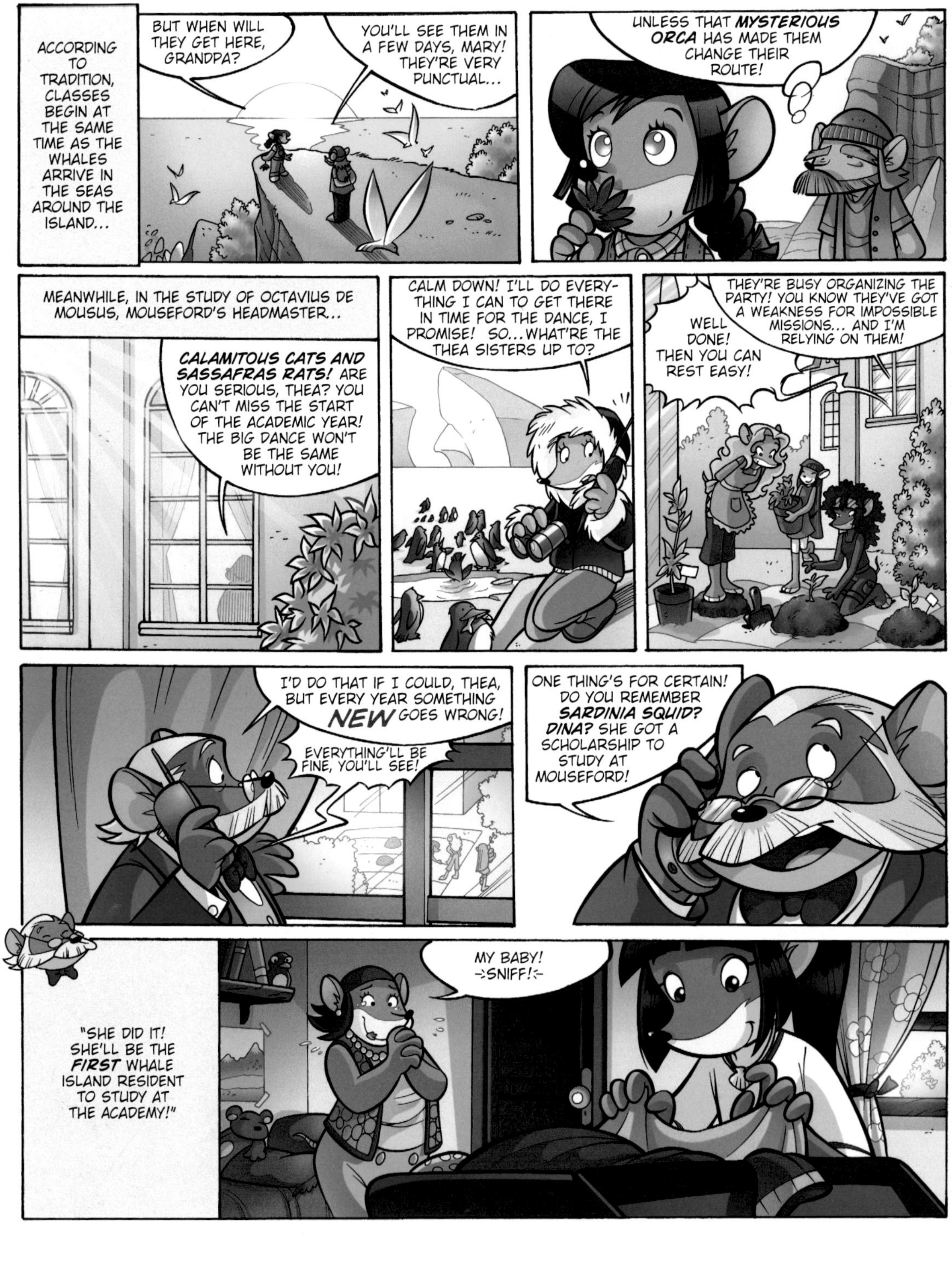
ACCORDING TO TRADITION, CLASSES BEGIN AT THE SAME TIME AS THE WHALES ARRIVE IN THE SEAS AROUND THE ISLAND...
BUT WHEN WILL THEY GET HERE, GRANDPA?
YOU'LL SEE THEM IN A FEW DAYS, MARY! THEY'RE VERY PUNCTUAL...
UNLESS THAT MYSTERIOUS ORCA HAS MADE THEM CHANGE THEIR ROUTE!
MEANWHILE, IN THE STUDY OF OCTAVIUS DE MOUSUS, MOUSEFORD'S HEADMASTER...
CALAMITOUS CATS AND SASSAFRAS RATS! ARE YOU SERIOUS, THEA? YOU CAN'T MISS THE START OF THE ACADEMIC YEAR! THE BIG DANCE WON'T BE THE SAME WITHOUT YOU!
CALM DOWN! I'LL DO EVERY-THING I CAN TO GET THERE IN TIME FOR THE DANCE, I PROMISE! SO...WHAT'RE THE THEA SISTERS UP TO?
THEY'RE BUSY ORGANIZING THE PARTY! YOU KNOW THEY'VE GOT A WEAKNESS FOR IMPOSSIBLE MISSIONS... AND I'M RELYING ON THEM!
WELL DONE! THEN YOU CAN REST EASY!
I'D DO THAT IF I COULD, THEA, BUT EVERY YEAR SOMETHING NEW GOES WRONG!
EVERYTHING'LL BE FINE, YOU'LL SEE!
ONE THING'S FOR CERTAIN! DO YOU REMEMBER SARDINIA SQUID? DINA? SHE GOT A SCHOLARSHIP TO STUDY AT MOUSEFORD!
"SHE DID IT! SHE'LL BE THE FIRST WHALE ISLAND RESIDENT TO STUDY AT THE ACADEMY!"
MY BABY! -SNIFF!-

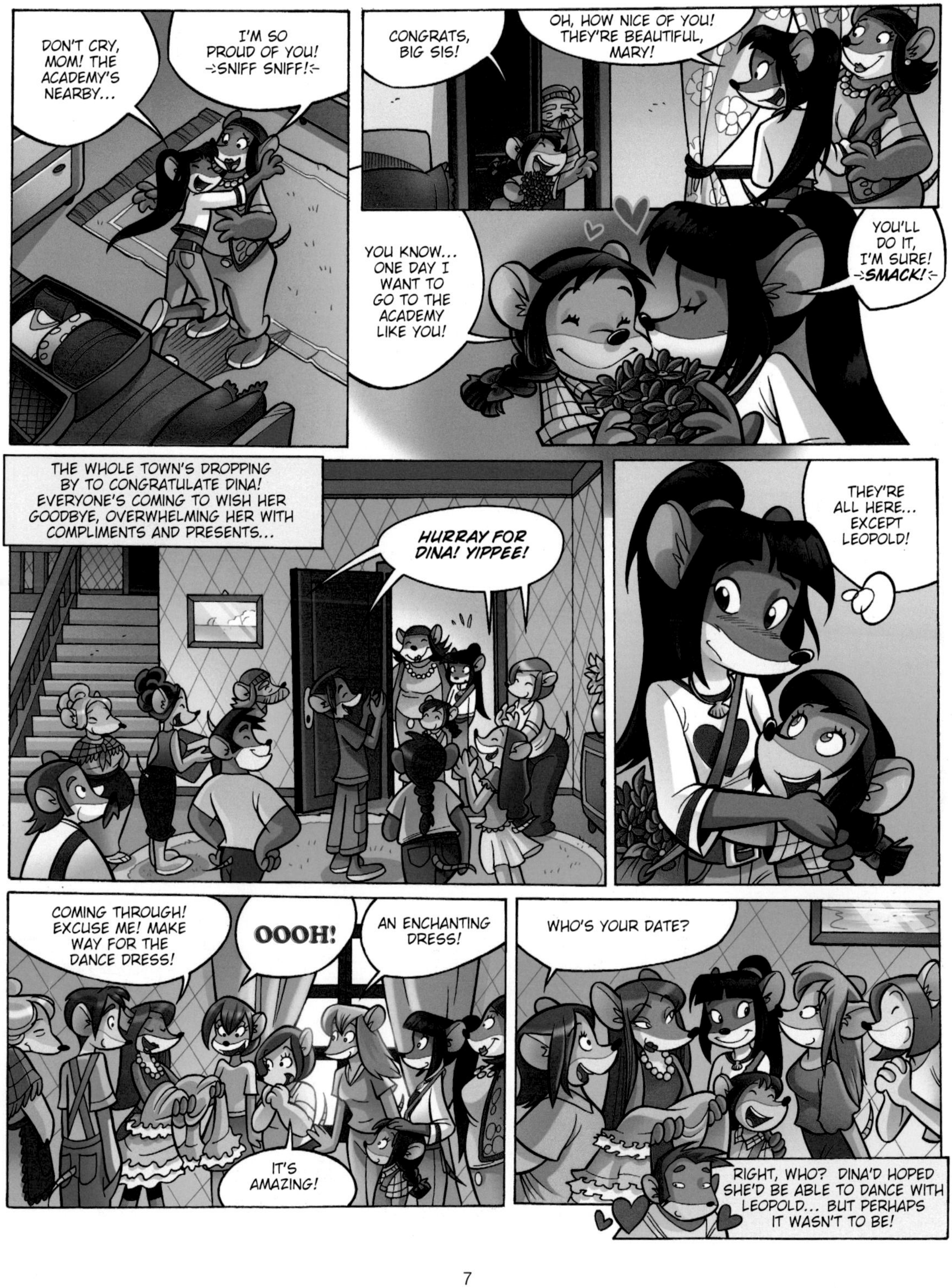
DON'T CRY, MOM! THE ACADEMY'S NEARBY...
I'M SO PROUD OF YOU! -SNIFF SNIFF!-
CONGRATS, BIG SIS!
OH, HOW NICE OF YOU! THEY'RE BEAUTIFUL, MARY!
YOU KNOW... ONE DAY I WANT TO GO TO THE ACADEMY LIKE YOU!
YOU'LL DO IT, I'M SURE! -SMACK!-
THE WHOLE TOWN'S DROPPING BY TO CONGRATULATE DINA! EVERYONE'S COMING TO WISH HER GOODBYE, OVERWHELMING HER WITH COMPLIMENTS AND PRESENTS...
HURRAY FOR DINA! YIPPEE!
THEY'RE ALL HERE... EXCEPT LEOPOLD!
COMING THROUGH! EXCUSE ME! MAKE WAY FOR THE DANCE DRESS!
OOOH!
AN ENCHANTING DRESS!
IT'S AMAZING!
WHO'S YOUR DATE?
RIGHT, WHO? DINA'D HOPED SHE'D BE ABLE TO DANCE WITH LEOPOLD... BUT PERHAPS IT WASN'T TO BE!

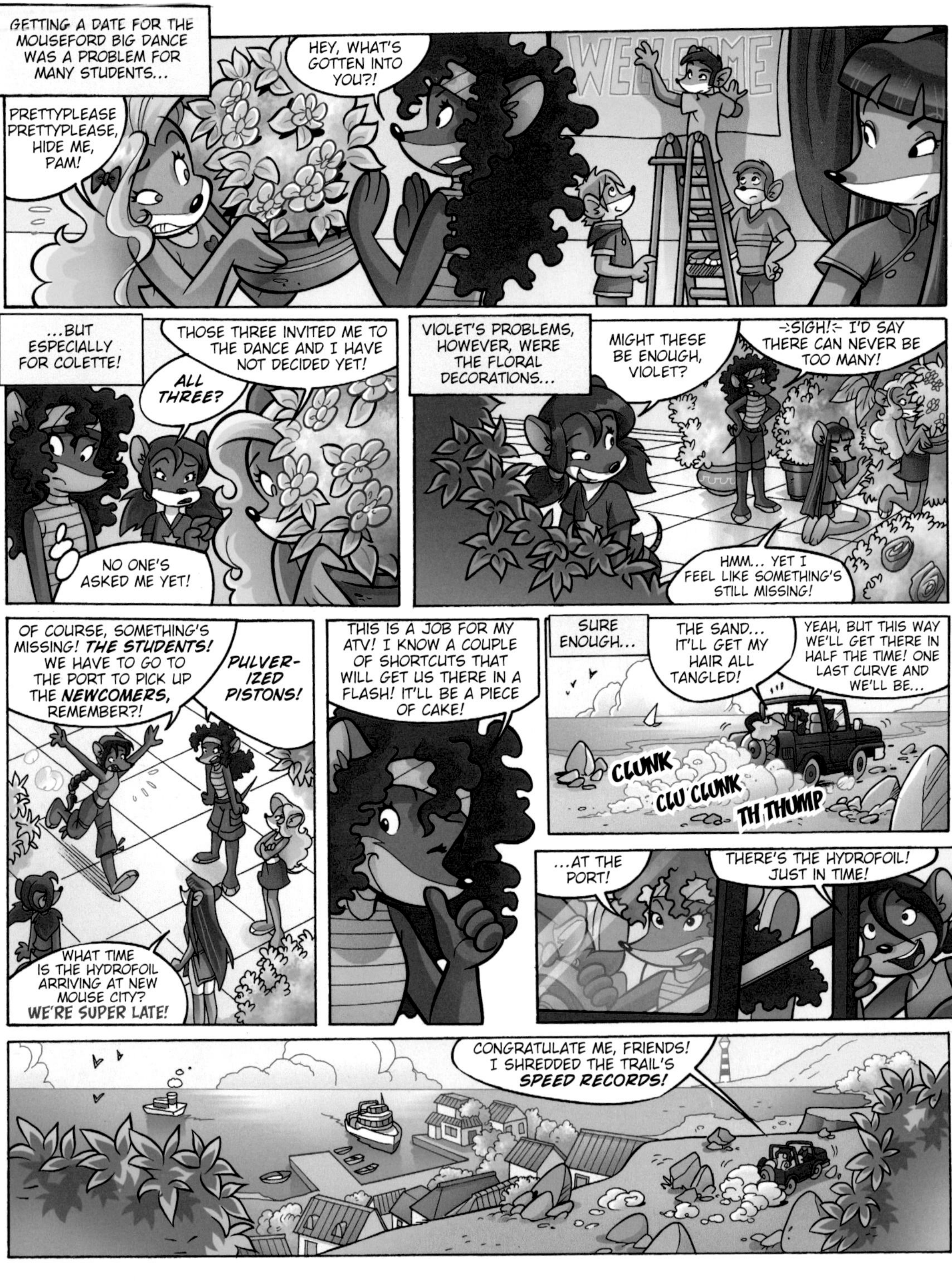

GETTING A DATE FOR THE MOUSEFORD BIG DANCE WAS A PROBLEM FOR MANY STUDENTS...
PRETTYPLEASE PRETTYPLEASE, HIDE ME, PAM!
HEY, WHAT'S GOTTEN INTO YOU?!
WELCOME
...BUT ESPECIALLY FOR COLETTE!
THOSE THREE INVITED ME TO THE DANCE AND I HAVE NOT DECIDED YET!
ALL THREE?
NO ONE'S ASKED ME YET!
VIOLET'S PROBLEMS, HOWEVER, WERE THE FLORAL DECORATIONS...
MIGHT THESE BE ENOUGH, VIOLET?
=SIGH!= I'D SAY THERE CAN NEVER BE TOO MANY!
HMM... YET I FEEL LIKE SOMETHING'S STILL MISSING!
OF COURSE, SOMETHING'S MISSING! THE STUDENTS! WE HAVE TO GO TO THE PORT TO PICK UP THE NEWCOMERS, REMEMBER?!
PULVERIZED PISTONS!
WHAT TIME IS THE HYDROFOIL ARRIVING AT NEW MOUSE CITY? WE'RE SUPER LATE!
THIS IS A JOB FOR MY ATV! I KNOW A COUPLE OF SHORTCUTS THAT WILL GET US THERE IN A FLASH! IT'LL BE A PIECE OF CAKE!
SURE ENOUGH...
THE SAND... IT'LL GET MY HAIR ALL TANGLED!
YEAH, BUT THIS WAY WE'LL GET THERE IN HALF THE TIME! ONE LAST CURVE AND WE'LL BE...
CLUNK
CLU CLUNK
TH THUMP
...AT THE PORT!
THERE'S THE HYDROFOIL! JUST IN TIME!
CONGRATULATE ME, FRIENDS! I SHREDDED THE TRAIL'S SPEED RECORDS!

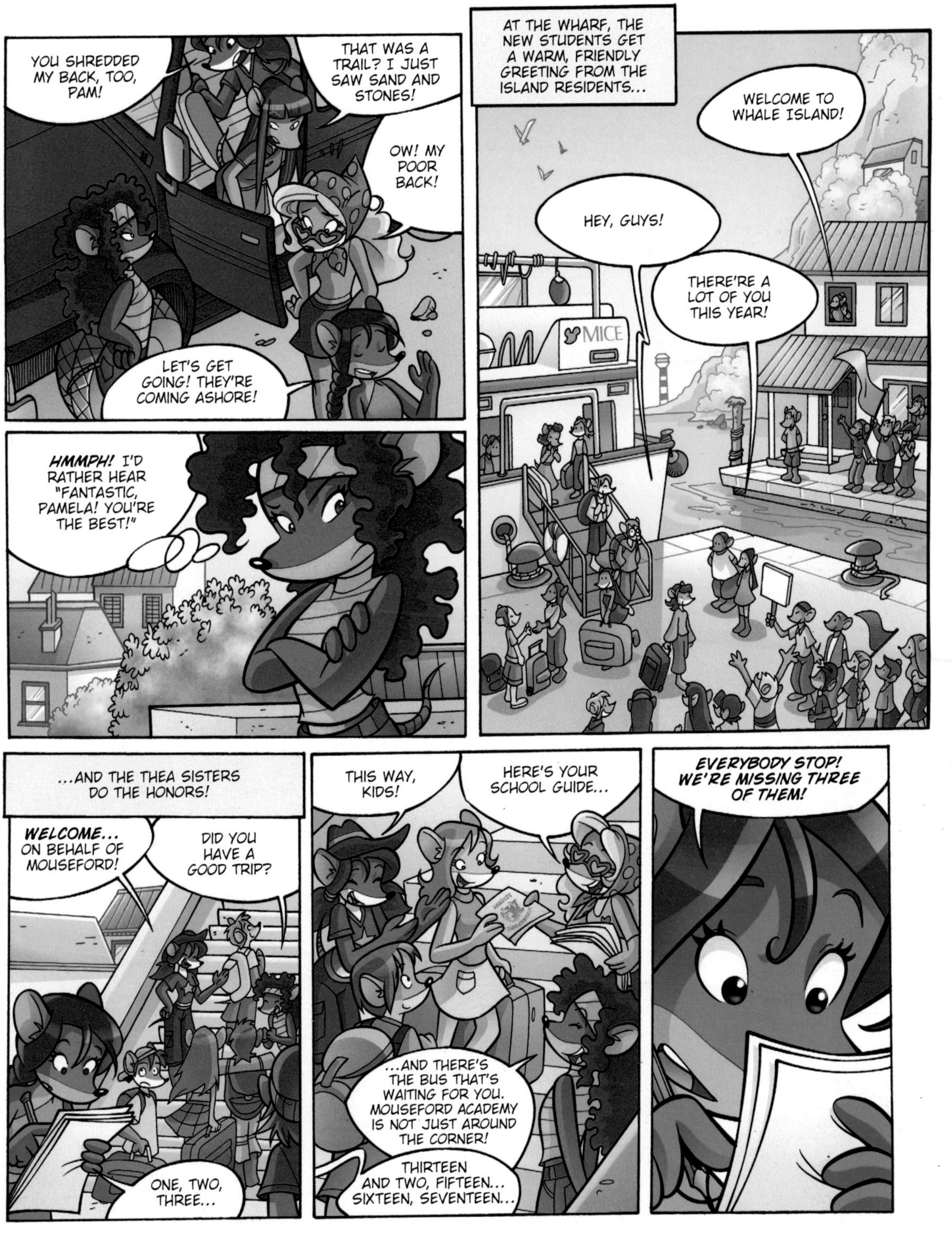
YOU SHREDDED MY BACK, TOO, PAM!
THAT WAS A TRAIL? I JUST SAW SAND AND STONES!
OW! MY POOR BACK!
LET'S GET GOING! THEY'RE COMING ASHORE!
HMMPH! I'D RATHER HEAR "FANTASTIC, PAMELA! YOU'RE THE BEST!"
AT THE WHARF, THE NEW STUDENTS GET A WARM, FRIENDLY GREETING FROM THE ISLAND RESIDENTS...
WELCOME TO WHALE ISLAND!
HEY, GUYS!
THERE'RE A LOT OF YOU THIS YEAR!
MICE
...AND THE THEA SISTERS DO THE HONORS!
WELCOME... ON BEHALF OF MOUSEFORD!
DID YOU HAVE A GOOD TRIP?
ONE, TWO, THREE...
THIS WAY, KIDS!
HERE'S YOUR SCHOOL GUIDE...
...AND THERE'S THE BUS THAT'S WAITING FOR YOU. MOUSEFORD ACADEMY IS NOT JUST AROUND THE CORNER!
THIRTEEN AND TWO, FIFTEEN... SIXTEEN, SEVENTEEN...
EVERYBODY STOP! WE'RE MISSING THREE OF THEM!

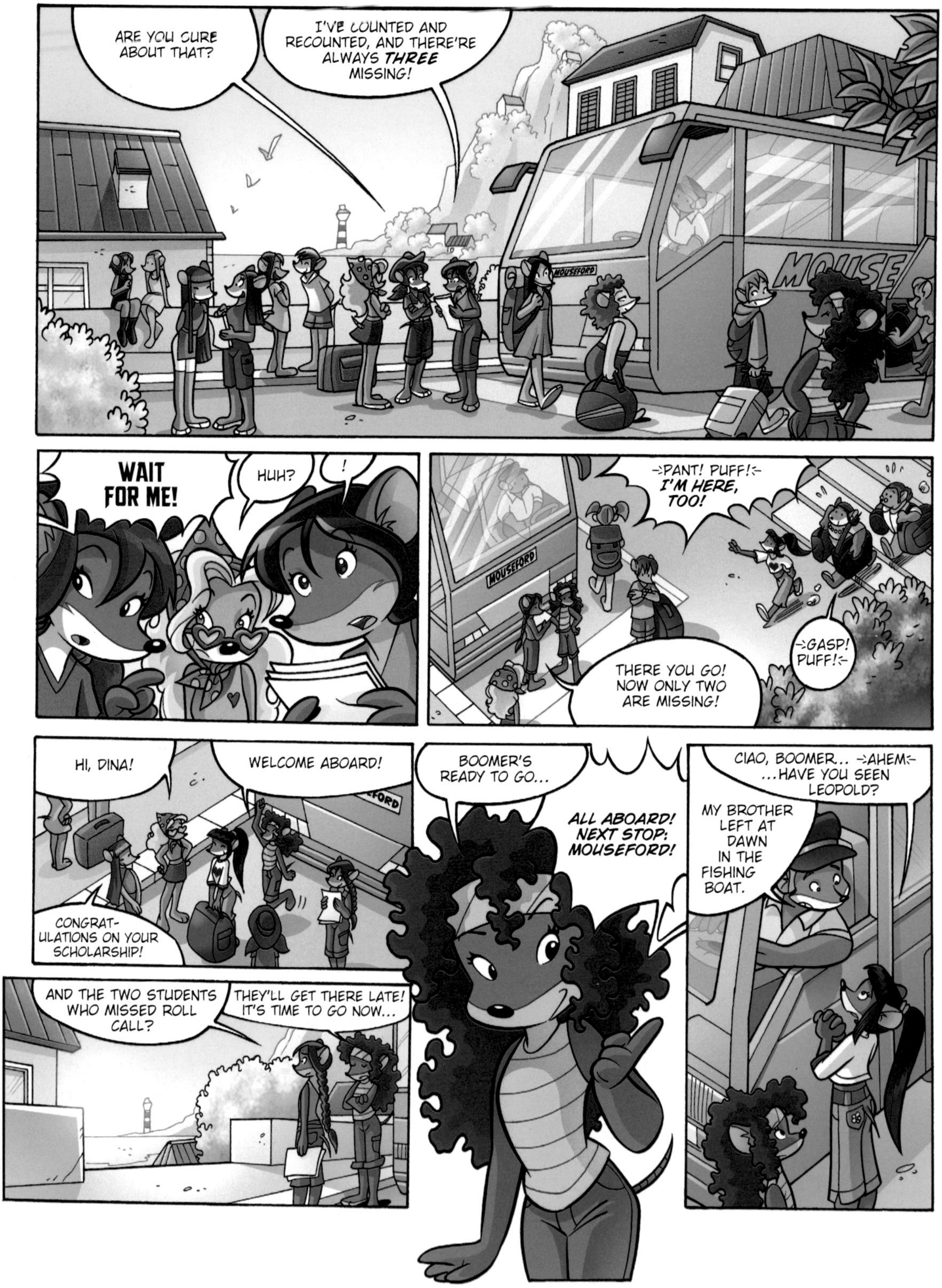
ARE YOU SURE ABOUT THAT?
I'VE COUNTED AND RECOUNTED, AND THERE'RE ALWAYS **THREE** MISSING!
MOUSEFORD
MOUSE
WAIT FOR ME!
HUH?
!
-PANT! PUFF!- **I'M HERE, TOO!**
MOUSEFORD
-GASP! PUFF!-
THERE YOU GO! NOW ONLY TWO ARE MISSING!
HI, DINA!
WELCOME ABOARD!
CONGRAT-ULATIONS ON YOUR SCHOLARSHIP!
BOOMER'S READY TO GO...
ALL ABOARD! NEXT STOP: MOUSEFORD!
CIAO, BOOMER... -AHEM- ...HAVE YOU SEEN LEOPOLD?
MY BROTHER LEFT AT DAWN IN THE FISHING BOAT.
AND THE TWO STUDENTS WHO MISSED ROLL CALL?
THEY'LL GET THERE LATE! IT'S TIME TO GO NOW...

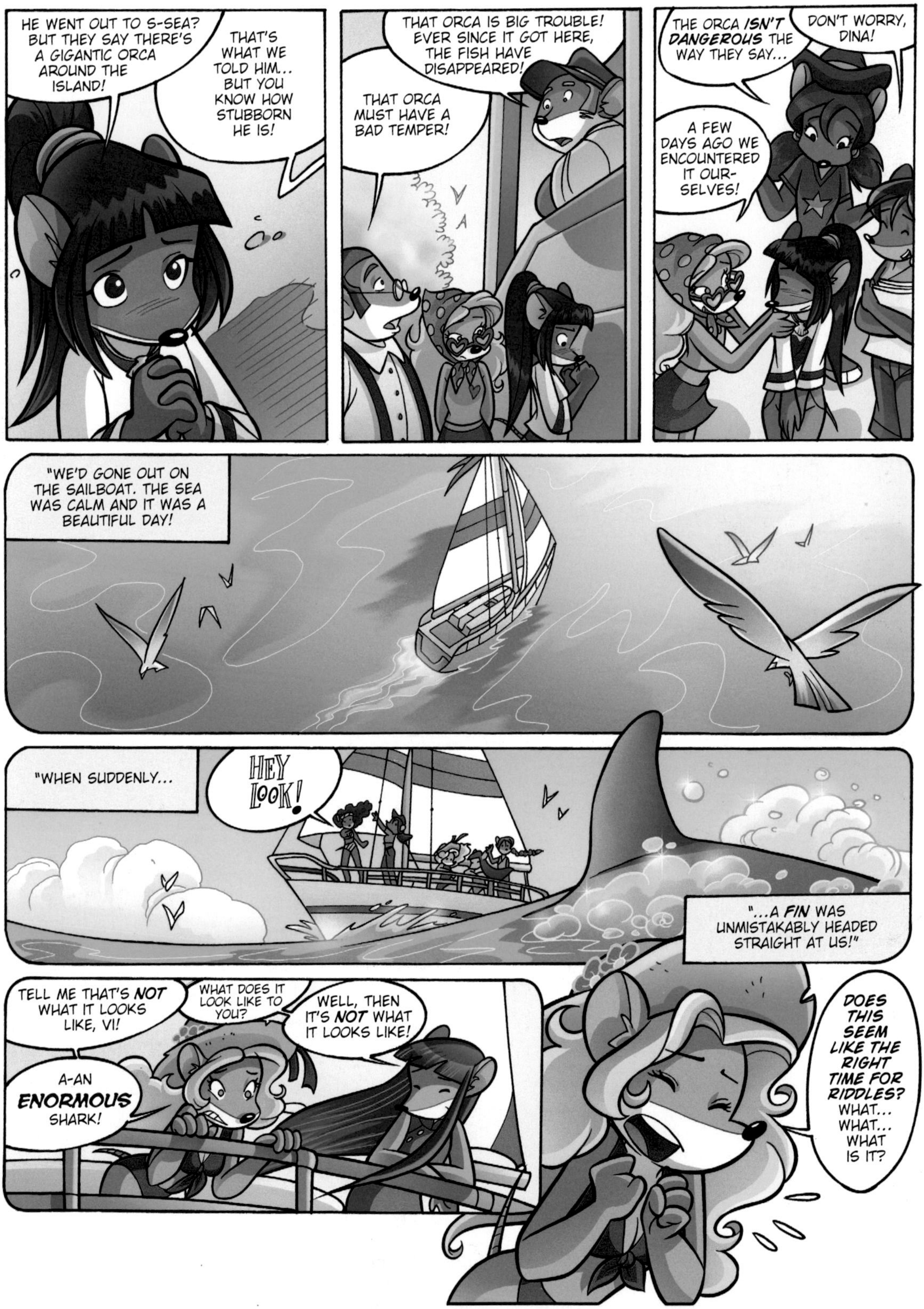
HE WENT OUT TO S-SEA? BUT THEY SAY THERE'S A GIGANTIC ORCA AROUND THE ISLAND!
THAT'S WHAT WE TOLD HIM... BUT YOU KNOW HOW STUBBORN HE IS!
THAT ORCA IS BIG TROUBLE! EVER SINCE IT GOT HERE, THE FISH HAVE DISAPPEARED!
THAT ORCA MUST HAVE A BAD TEMPER!
THE ORCA ISN'T DANGEROUS THE WAY THEY SAY...
DON'T WORRY, DINA!
A FEW DAYS AGO WE ENCOUNTERED IT OUR-SELVES!
"WE'D GONE OUT ON THE SAILBOAT. THE SEA WAS CALM AND IT WAS A BEAUTIFUL DAY!
"WHEN SUDDENLY...
HEY LOOK!
"...A FIN WAS UNMISTAKABLY HEADED STRAIGHT AT US!"
TELL ME THAT'S NOT WHAT IT LOOKS LIKE, VI!
WHAT DOES IT LOOK LIKE TO YOU?
WELL, THEN IT'S NOT WHAT IT LOOKS LIKE!
A-AN ENORMOUS SHARK!
DOES THIS SEEM LIKE THE RIGHT TIME FOR RIDDLES? WHAT... WHAT... WHAT IS IT?

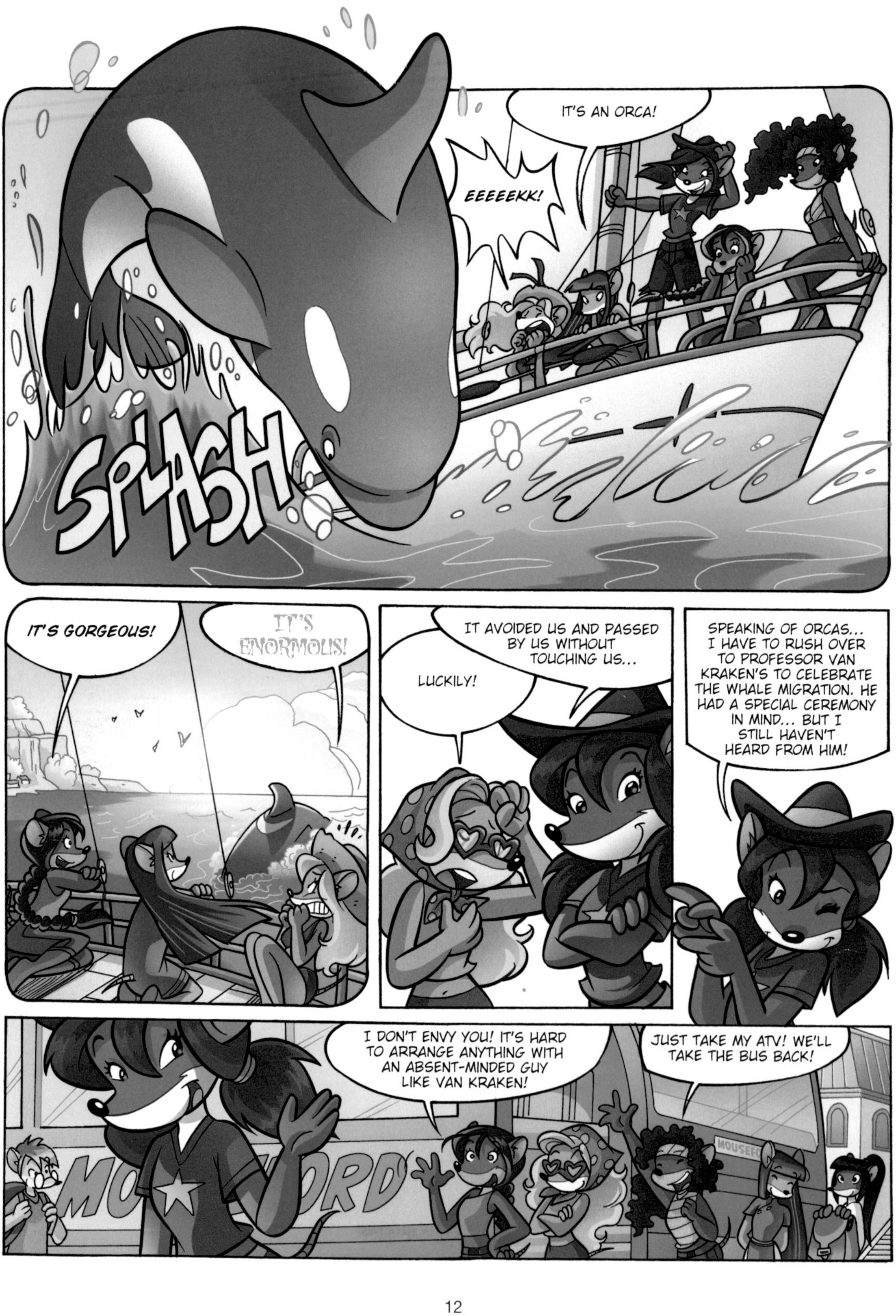
EEEEEKK!
IT'S AN ORCA!
SPLASH
IT'S GORGEOUS!
IT'S ENORMOUS!
IT AVOIDED US AND PASSED BY US WITHOUT TOUCHING US...
LUCKILY!
SPEAKING OF ORCAS... I HAVE TO RUSH OVER TO PROFESSOR VAN KRAKEN'S TO CELEBRATE THE WHALE MIGRATION. HE HAD A SPECIAL CEREMONY IN MIND... BUT I STILL HAVEN'T HEARD FROM HIM!
I DON'T ENVY YOU! IT'S HARD TO ARRANGE ANYTHING WITH AN ABSENT-MINDED GUY LIKE VAN KRAKEN!
JUST TAKE MY ATV! WE'LL TAKE THE BUS BACK!

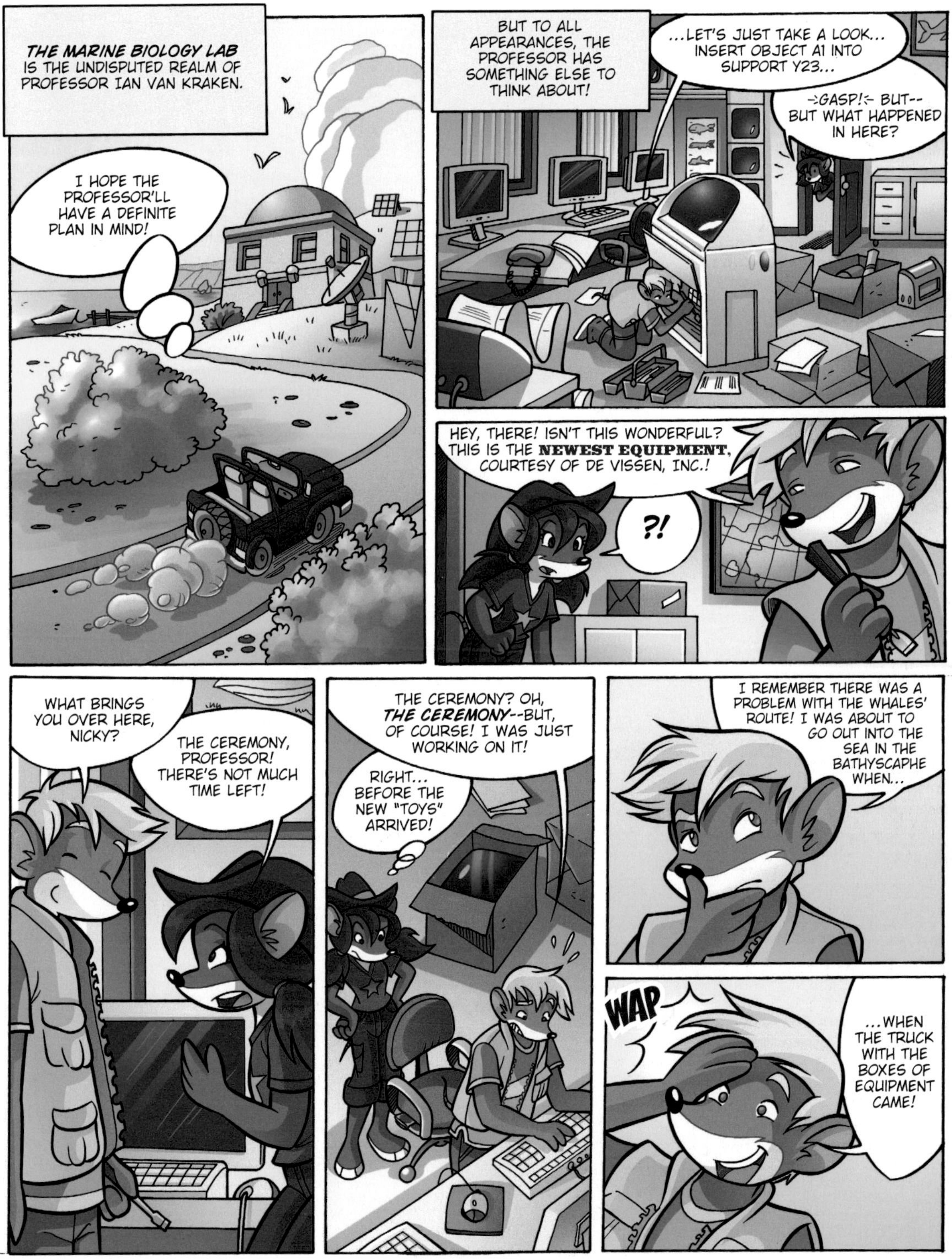
THE MARINE BIOLOGY LAB IS THE UNDISPUTED REALM OF PROFESSOR IAN VAN KRAKEN.
I HOPE THE PROFESSOR'LL HAVE A DEFINITE PLAN IN MIND!
BUT TO ALL APPEARANCES, THE PROFESSOR HAS SOMETHING ELSE TO THINK ABOUT!
...LET'S JUST TAKE A LOOK... INSERT OBJECT A1 INTO SUPPORT Y23...
-GASP!- BUT-- BUT WHAT HAPPENED IN HERE?
HEY, THERE! ISN'T THIS WONDERFUL? THIS IS THE NEWEST EQUIPMENT, COURTESY OF DE VISSEN, INC.!
?!
WHAT BRINGS YOU OVER HERE, NICKY?
THE CEREMONY, PROFESSOR! THERE'S NOT MUCH TIME LEFT!
THE CEREMONY? OH, THE CEREMONY--BUT, OF COURSE! I WAS JUST WORKING ON IT!
RIGHT... BEFORE THE NEW "TOYS" ARRIVED!
I REMEMBER THERE WAS A PROBLEM WITH THE WHALES' ROUTE! I WAS ABOUT TO GO OUT INTO THE SEA IN THE BATHYSCAPHE WHEN...
WAP
...WHEN THE TRUCK WITH THE BOXES OF EQUIPMENT CAME!

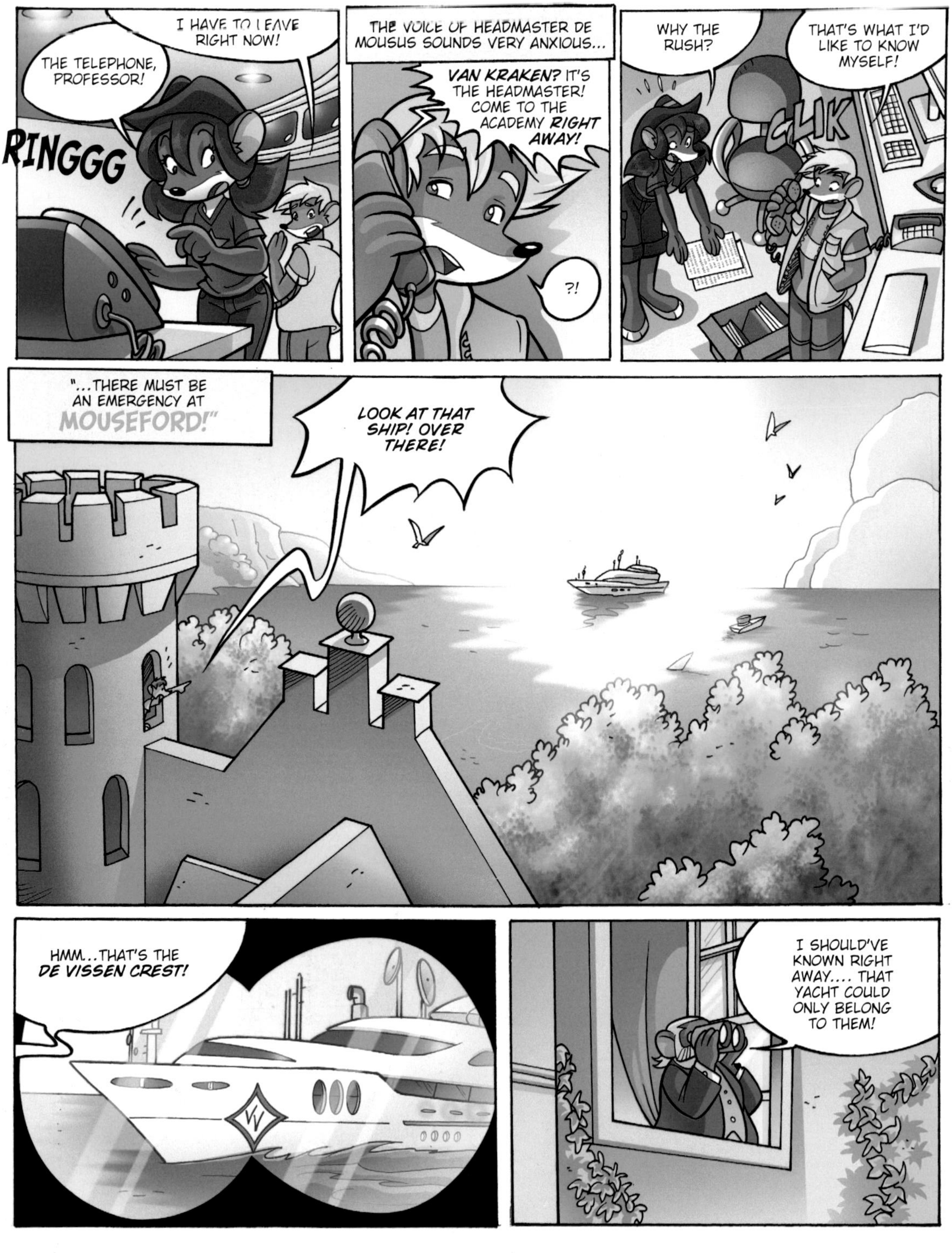

RINGGG
THE TELEPHONE, PROFESSOR!
I HAVE TO LEAVE RIGHT NOW!
THE VOICE OF HEADMASTER DE MOUSUS SOUNDS VERY ANXIOUS...
VAN KRAKEN? IT'S THE HEADMASTER! COME TO THE ACADEMY RIGHT AWAY!
?!
WHY THE RUSH?
THAT'S WHAT I'D LIKE TO KNOW MYSELF!
CLIK
"...THERE MUST BE AN EMERGENCY AT MOUSEFORD!"
LOOK AT THAT SHIP! OVER THERE!
HMM...THAT'S THE DE VISSEN CREST!
I SHOULD'VE KNOWN RIGHT AWAY.... THAT YACHT COULD ONLY BELONG TO THEM!

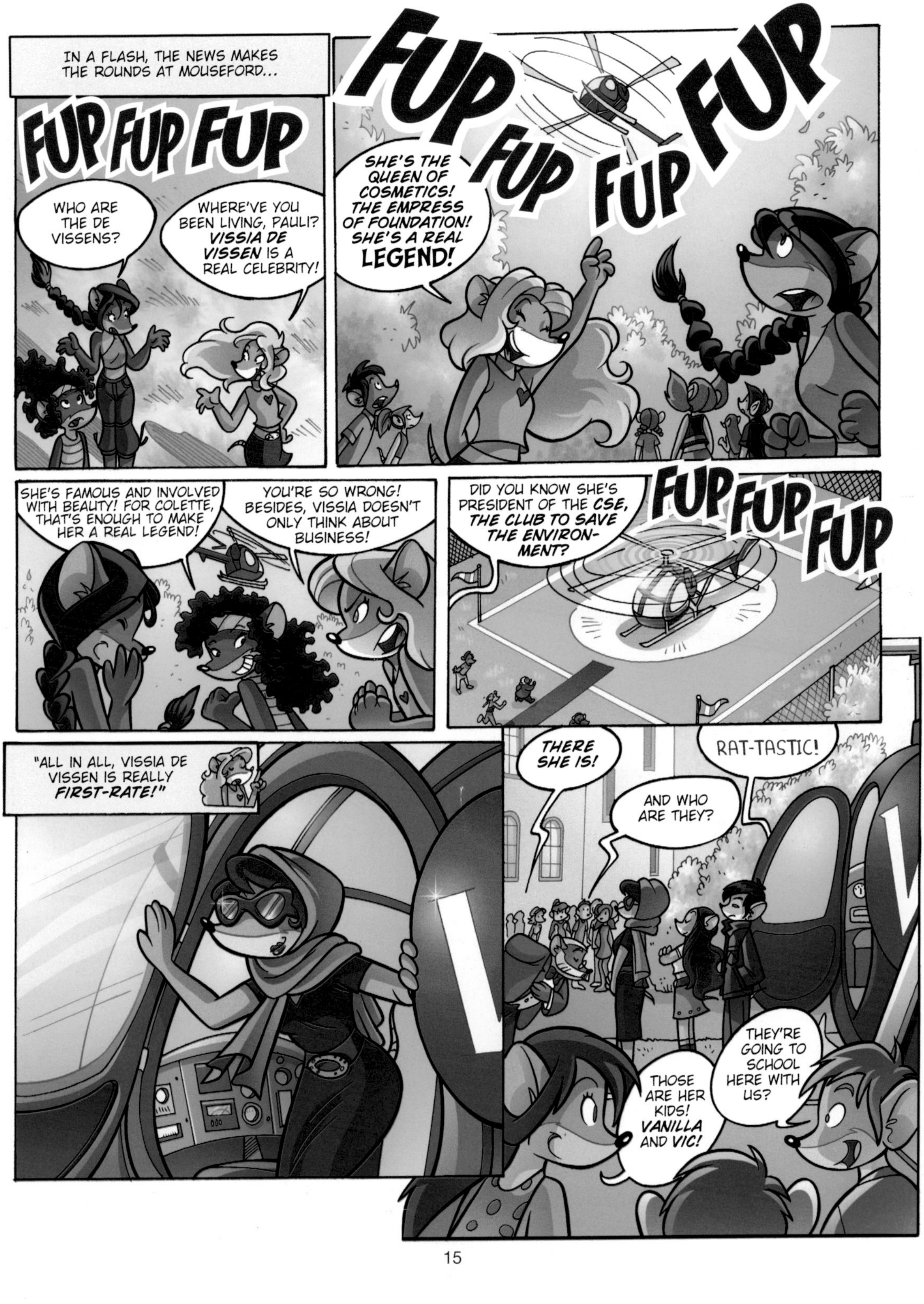

IN A FLASH, THE NEWS MAKES THE ROUNDS AT MOUSEFORD...
FUP FUP FUP
WHO ARE THE DE VISSENS?
WHERE'VE YOU BEEN LIVING, PAULI? VISSIA DE VISSEN IS A REAL CELEBRITY!
FUP FUP FUP FUP
SHE'S THE QUEEN OF COSMETICS! THE EMPRESS OF FOUNDATION! SHE'S A REAL LEGEND!
SHE'S FAMOUS AND INVOLVED WITH BEAUTY! FOR COLETTE, THAT'S ENOUGH TO MAKE HER A REAL LEGEND!
YOU'RE SO WRONG! BESIDES, VISSIA DOESN'T ONLY THINK ABOUT BUSINESS!
DID YOU KNOW SHE'S PRESIDENT OF THE CSE, THE CLUB TO SAVE THE ENVIRONMENT?
FUP FUP FUP
"ALL IN ALL, VISSIA DE VISSEN IS REALLY FIRST-RATE!"
THERE SHE IS!
RAT-TASTIC!
AND WHO ARE THEY?
THOSE ARE HER KIDS! VANILLA AND VIC!
THEY'RE GOING TO SCHOOL HERE WITH US?

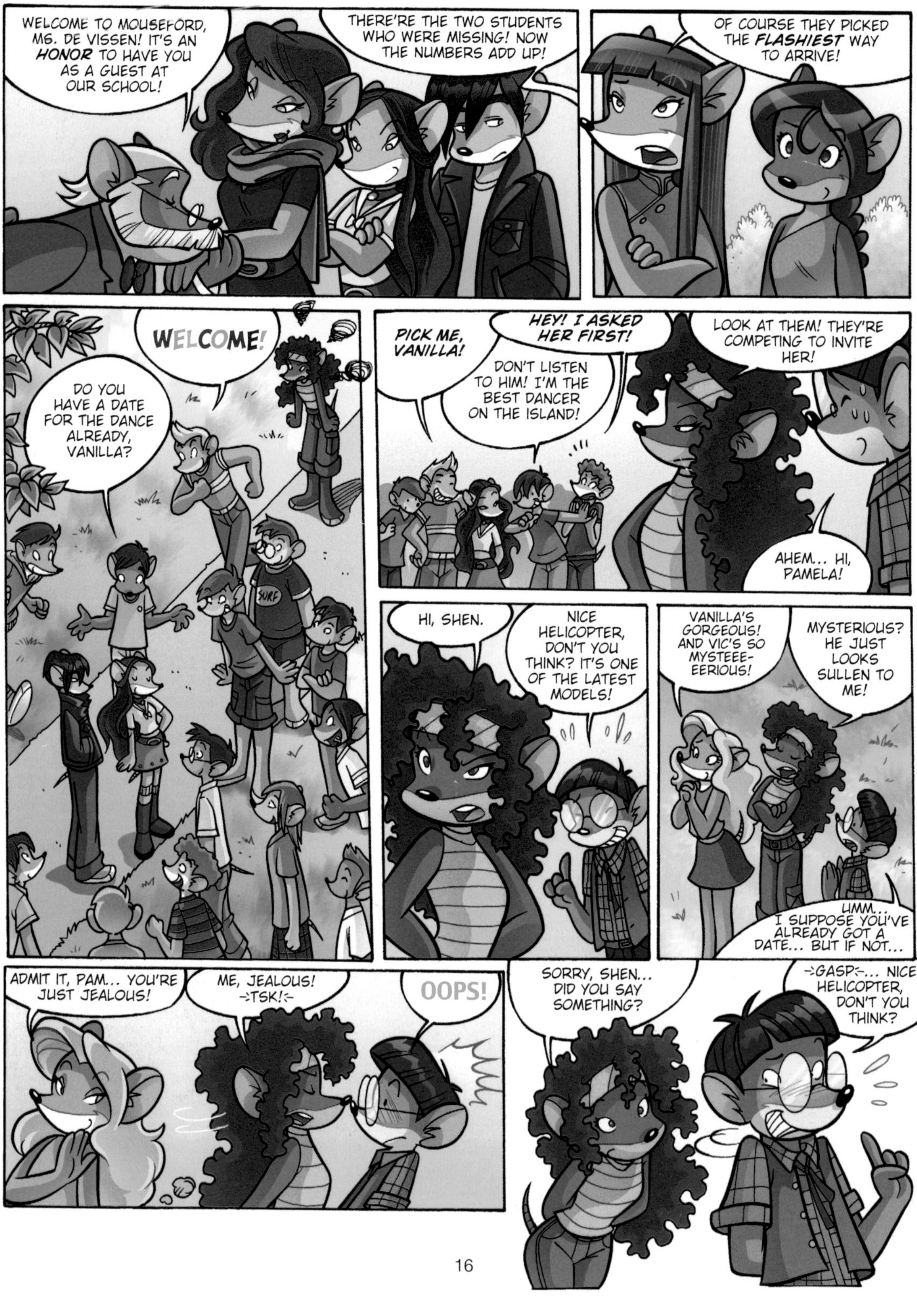
WELCOME TO MOUSEFORD, MS. DE VISSEN! IT'S AN **HONOR** TO HAVE YOU AS A GUEST AT OUR SCHOOL!
THERE'RE THE TWO STUDENTS WHO WERE MISSING! NOW THE NUMBERS ADD UP!
OF COURSE THEY PICKED THE **FLASHIEST** WAY TO ARRIVE!
WELCOME!
DO YOU HAVE A DATE FOR THE DANCE ALREADY, VANILLA?
PICK ME, VANILLA!
HEY! I ASKED HER FIRST!
DON'T LISTEN TO HIM! I'M THE BEST DANCER ON THE ISLAND!
LOOK AT THEM! THEY'RE COMPETING TO INVITE HER!
AHEM... HI, PAMELA!
HI, SHEN.
NICE HELICOPTER, DON'T YOU THINK? IT'S ONE OF THE LATEST MODELS!
VANILLA'S GORGEOUS! AND VIC'S SO MYSTEEE-EERIOUS!
MYSTERIOUS? HE JUST LOOKS SULLEN TO ME!
UMM... I SUPPOSE YOU'VE ALREADY GOT A DATE... BUT IF NOT...
ADMIT IT, PAM... YOU'RE JUST JEALOUS!
ME, JEALOUS! -TSK!-
OOPS!
SORRY, SHEN... DID YOU SAY SOMETHING?
-GASP-... NICE HELICOPTER, DON'T YOU THINK?

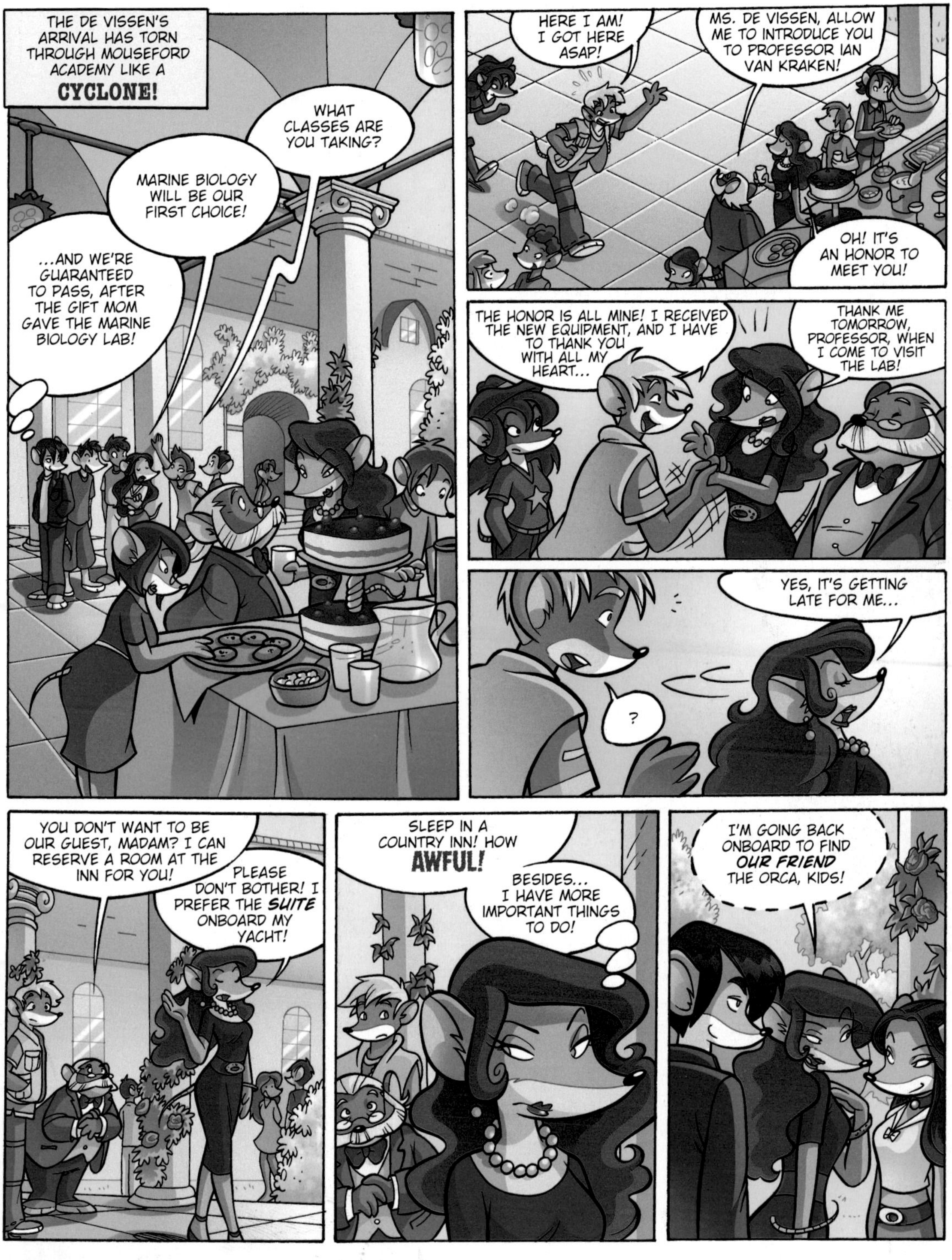
THE DE VISSEN'S ARRIVAL HAS TORN THROUGH MOUSEFORD ACADEMY LIKE A CYCLONE!
WHAT CLASSES ARE YOU TAKING?
MARINE BIOLOGY WILL BE OUR FIRST CHOICE!
...AND WE'RE GUARANTEED TO PASS, AFTER THE GIFT MOM GAVE THE MARINE BIOLOGY LAB!
HERE I AM! I GOT HERE ASAP!
MS. DE VISSEN, ALLOW ME TO INTRODUCE YOU TO PROFESSOR IAN VAN KRAKEN!
OH! IT'S AN HONOR TO MEET YOU!
THE HONOR IS ALL MINE! I RECEIVED THE NEW EQUIPMENT, AND I HAVE TO THANK YOU WITH ALL MY HEART...
THANK ME TOMORROW, PROFESSOR, WHEN I COME TO VISIT THE LAB!
YES, IT'S GETTING LATE FOR ME...
?
YOU DON'T WANT TO BE OUR GUEST, MADAM? I CAN RESERVE A ROOM AT THE INN FOR YOU!
PLEASE DON'T BOTHER! I PREFER THE SUITE ONBOARD MY YACHT!
SLEEP IN A COUNTRY INN! HOW AWFUL!
BESIDES... I HAVE MORE IMPORTANT THINGS TO DO!
I'M GOING BACK ONBOARD TO FIND OUR FRIEND THE ORCA, KIDS!

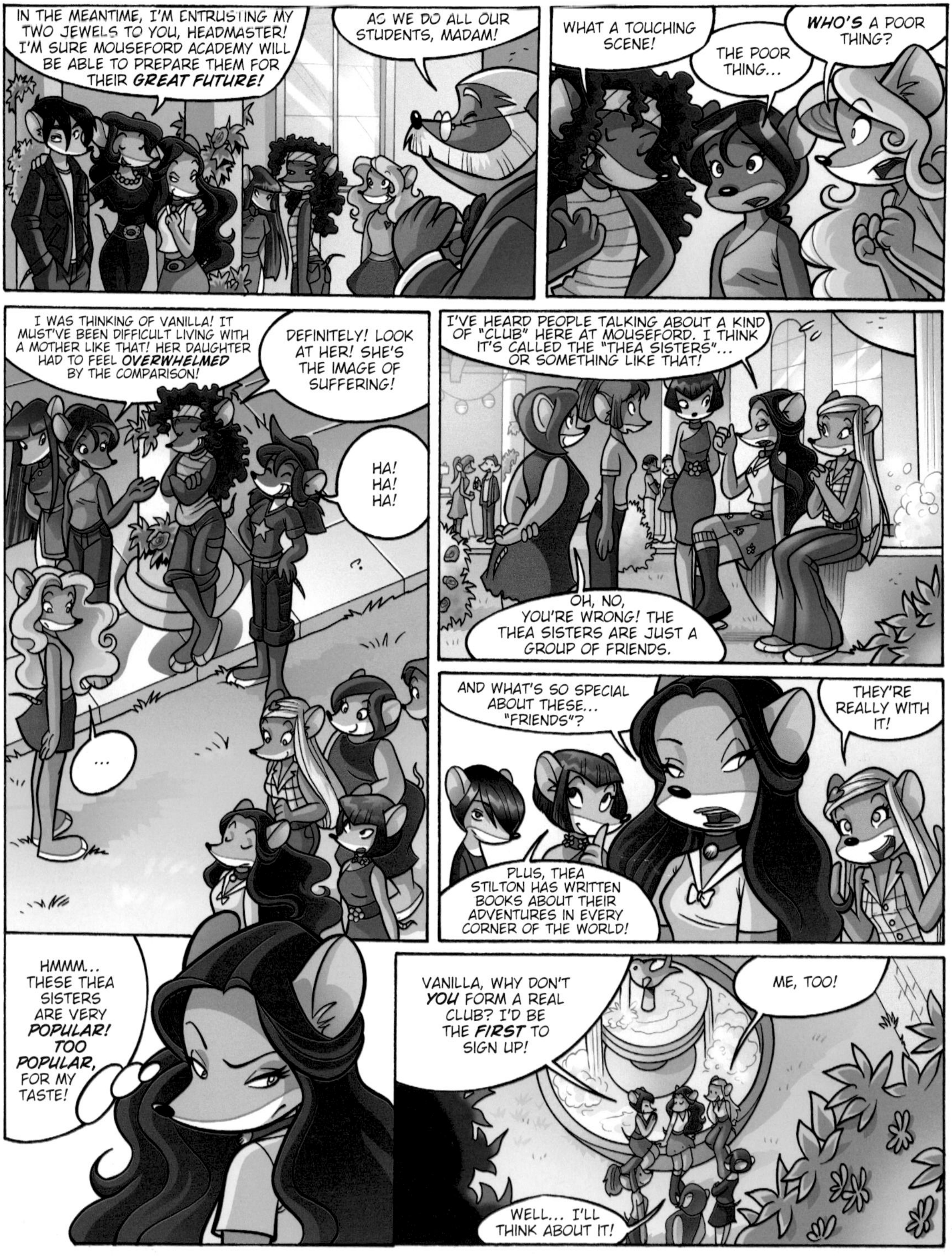
IN THE MEANTIME, I'M ENTRUSTING MY TWO JEWELS TO YOU, HEADMASTER! I'M SURE MOUSEFORD ACADEMY WILL BE ABLE TO PREPARE THEM FOR THEIR GREAT FUTURE!
AS WE DO ALL OUR STUDENTS, MADAM!
WHAT A TOUCHING SCENE!
THE POOR THING...
WHO'S A POOR THING?
I WAS THINKING OF VANILLA! IT MUST'VE BEEN DIFFICULT LIVING WITH A MOTHER LIKE THAT! HER DAUGHTER HAD TO FEEL OVERWHELMED BY THE COMPARISON!
DEFINITELY! LOOK AT HER! SHE'S THE IMAGE OF SUFFERING!
HA! HA! HA!
...
I'VE HEARD PEOPLE TALKING ABOUT A KIND OF "CLUB" HERE AT MOUSEFORD. I THINK IT'S CALLED THE "THEA SISTERS"... OR SOMETHING LIKE THAT!
OH, NO, YOU'RE WRONG! THE THEA SISTERS ARE JUST A GROUP OF FRIENDS.
AND WHAT'S SO SPECIAL ABOUT THESE... "FRIENDS"?
THEY'RE REALLY WITH IT!
PLUS, THEA STILTON HAS WRITTEN BOOKS ABOUT THEIR ADVENTURES IN EVERY CORNER OF THE WORLD!
HMMM... THESE THEA SISTERS ARE VERY POPULAR! TOO POPULAR, FOR MY TASTE!
VANILLA, WHY DON'T YOU FORM A REAL CLUB? I'D BE THE FIRST TO SIGN UP!
ME, TOO!
WELL... I'LL THINK ABOUT IT!

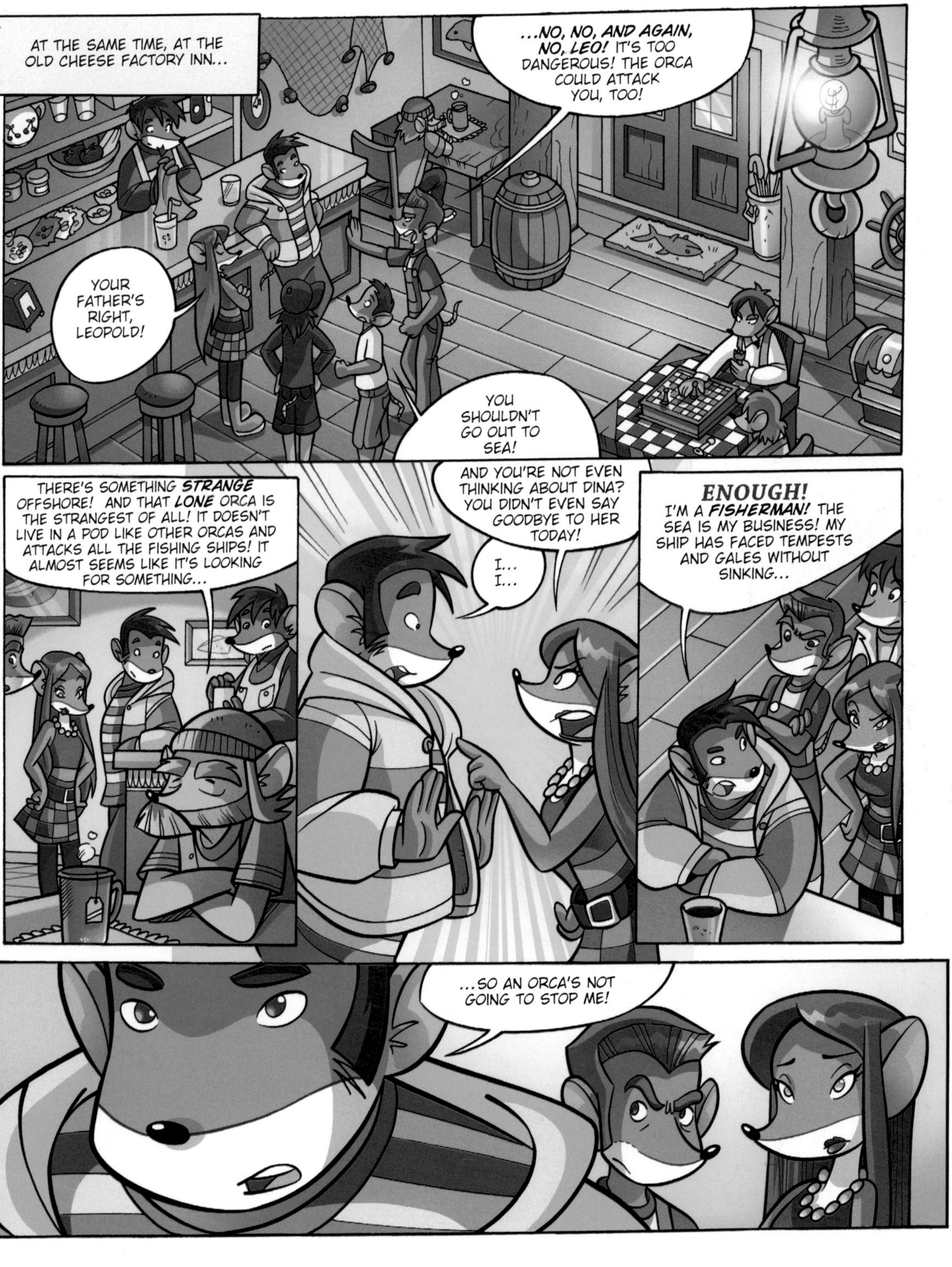
AT THE SAME TIME, AT THE OLD CHEESE FACTORY INN...
...NO, NO, AND AGAIN, NO, LEO! IT'S TOO DANGEROUS! THE ORCA COULD ATTACK YOU, TOO!
YOUR FATHER'S RIGHT, LEOPOLD!
YOU SHOULDN'T GO OUT TO SEA!
THERE'S SOMETHING STRANGE OFFSHORE! AND THAT LONE ORCA IS THE STRANGEST OF ALL! IT DOESN'T LIVE IN A POD LIKE OTHER ORCAS AND ATTACKS ALL THE FISHING SHIPS! IT ALMOST SEEMS LIKE IT'S LOOKING FOR SOMETHING...
AND YOU'RE NOT EVEN THINKING ABOUT DINA? YOU DIDN'T EVEN SAY GOODBYE TO HER TODAY!
I... I...
ENOUGH! I'M A FISHERMAN! THE SEA IS MY BUSINESS! MY SHIP HAS FACED TEMPESTS AND GALES WITHOUT SINKING...
...SO AN ORCA'S NOT GOING TO STOP ME!

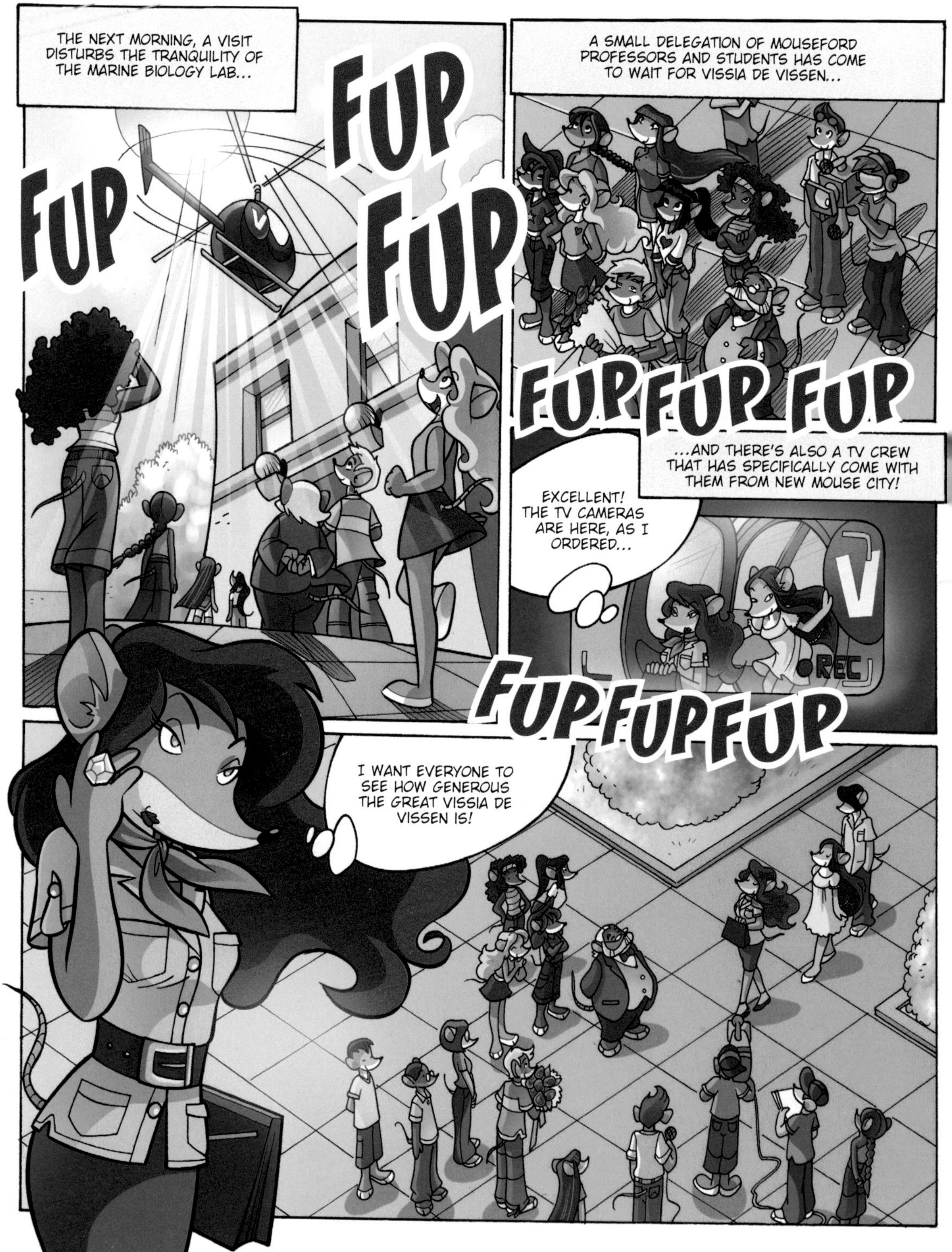
THE NEXT MORNING, A VISIT DISTURBS THE TRANQUILITY OF THE MARINE BIOLOGY LAB...
FUP
FUP
FUP
A SMALL DELEGATION OF MOUSEFORD PROFESSORS AND STUDENTS HAS COME TO WAIT FOR VISSIA DE VISSEN...
FUP FUP FUP
...AND THERE'S ALSO A TV CREW THAT HAS SPECIFICALLY COME WITH THEM FROM NEW MOUSE CITY!
EXCELLENT! THE TV CAMERAS ARE HERE, AS I ORDERED...
V
REC
FUP FUP FUP
I WANT EVERYONE TO SEE HOW GENEROUS THE GREAT VISSIA DE VISSEN IS!

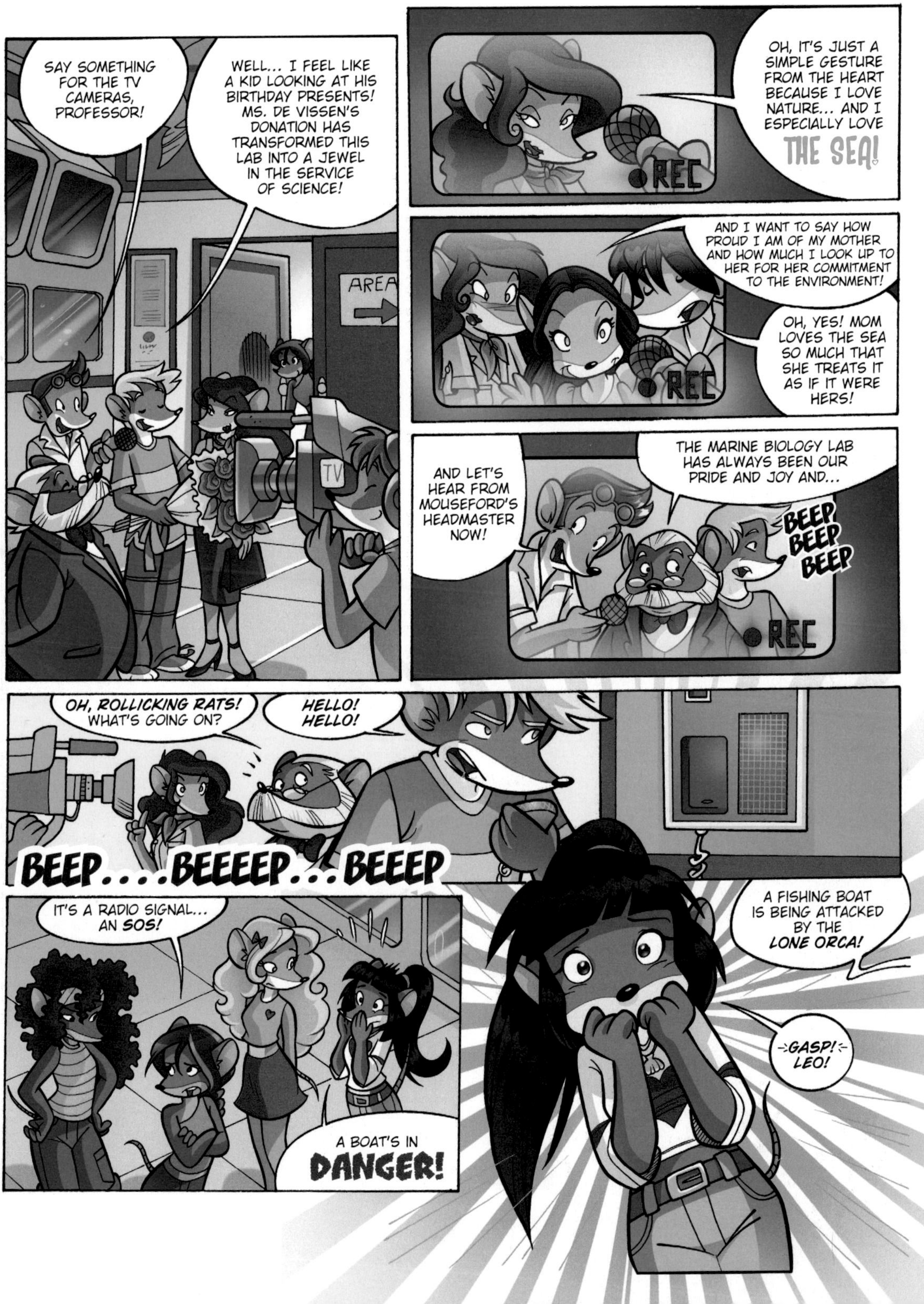
SAY SOMETHING FOR THE TV CAMERAS, PROFESSOR!
WELL... I FEEL LIKE A KID LOOKING AT HIS BIRTHDAY PRESENTS! MS. DE VISSEN'S DONATION HAS TRANSFORMED THIS LAB INTO A JEWEL IN THE SERVICE OF SCIENCE!
AREA
TV
REC
OH, IT'S JUST A SIMPLE GESTURE FROM THE HEART BECAUSE I LOVE NATURE... AND I ESPECIALLY LOVE THE SEA!
AND I WANT TO SAY HOW PROUD I AM OF MY MOTHER AND HOW MUCH I LOOK UP TO HER FOR HER COMMITMENT TO THE ENVIRONMENT!
OH, YES! MOM LOVES THE SEA SO MUCH THAT SHE TREATS IT AS IF IT WERE HERS!
REC
AND LET'S HEAR FROM MOUSEFORD'S HEADMASTER NOW!
THE MARINE BIOLOGY LAB HAS ALWAYS BEEN OUR PRIDE AND JOY AND...
BEEP BEEP BEEP
REC
OH, ROLLICKING RATS! WHAT'S GOING ON?
HELLO! HELLO!
BEEP....BEEEEP...BEEEP
IT'S A RADIO SIGNAL... AN SOS!
A BOAT'S IN DANGER!
A FISHING BOAT IS BEING ATTACKED BY THE LONE ORCA!
GASP! LEO!

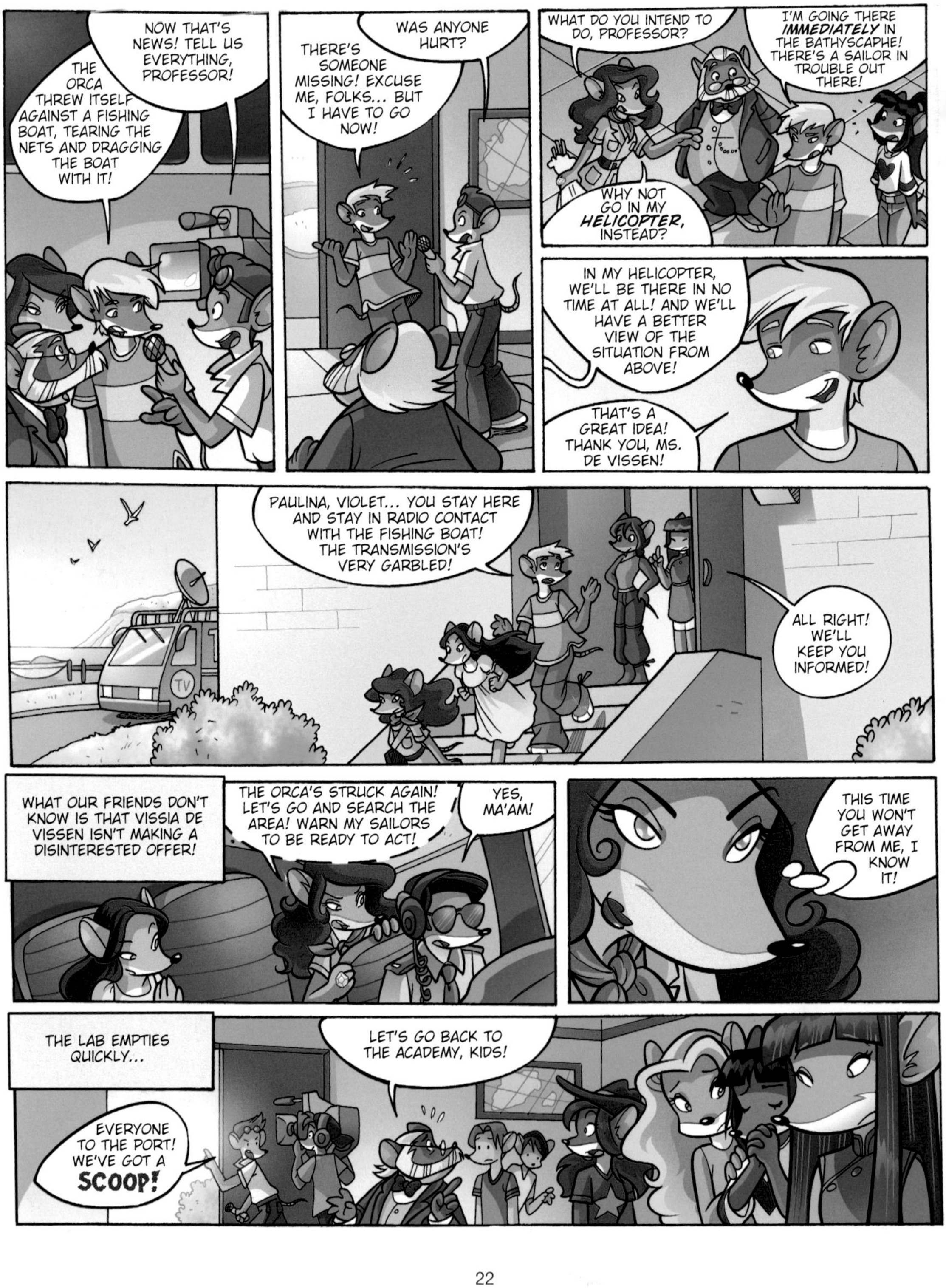
NOW THAT'S NEWS! TELL US EVERYTHING, PROFESSOR!
THE ORCA THREW ITSELF AGAINST A FISHING BOAT, TEARING THE NETS AND DRAGGING THE BOAT WITH IT!
WAS ANYONE HURT?
THERE'S SOMEONE MISSING! EXCUSE ME, FOLKS... BUT I HAVE TO GO NOW!
WHAT DO YOU INTEND TO DO, PROFESSOR?
I'M GOING THERE IMMEDIATELY IN THE BATHYSCAPHE! THERE'S A SAILOR IN TROUBLE OUT THERE!
WHY NOT GO IN MY HELICOPTER, INSTEAD?
IN MY HELICOPTER, WE'LL BE THERE IN NO TIME AT ALL! AND WE'LL HAVE A BETTER VIEW OF THE SITUATION FROM ABOVE!
THAT'S A GREAT IDEA! THANK YOU, MS. DE VISSEN!
PAULINA, VIOLET... YOU STAY HERE AND STAY IN RADIO CONTACT WITH THE FISHING BOAT! THE TRANSMISSION'S VERY GARBLED!
ALL RIGHT! WE'LL KEEP YOU INFORMED!
WHAT OUR FRIENDS DON'T KNOW IS THAT VISSIA DE VISSEN ISN'T MAKING A DISINTERESTED OFFER!
THE ORCA'S STRUCK AGAIN! LET'S GO AND SEARCH THE AREA! WARN MY SAILORS TO BE READY TO ACT!
YES, MA'AM!
THIS TIME YOU WON'T GET AWAY FROM ME, I KNOW IT!
THE LAB EMPTIES QUICKLY...
LET'S GO BACK TO THE ACADEMY, KIDS!
EVERYONE TO THE PORT! WE'VE GOT A SCOOP!

HURRY, PROFESSOR! **WE'RE TAKING OFF!**

FUP FUP FÚP

IS EVERYTHING OKAY, DINA?

WHY AREN'T YOU GOING BACK TO MOUSEFORD WITH EVERYONE?

I... I CAN'T!

THE SHIP THAT WAS ATTACKED COULD BE LEOPOLD'S!

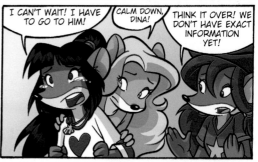

I CAN'T WAIT! I HAVE TO GO TO HIM!

CALM DOWN, DINA!

THINK IT OVER! WE DON'T HAVE EXACT INFORMATION YET!

LISTEN! THE NAME OF THE FISHING BOAT THAT WAS ATTACKED IS... *PROVOLONE II!* DOESN'T THAT TELL YOU SOMETHING?

THAT'S *LEO'S!* I KNEW IT! *LET ME GO!*

SLOW DOWN! YOU CAN'T BE THINKING OF GETTING TO HIM BY SWIMMING THERE?

WELL, THERE MIGHT BE A WAY...

WE COULD USE VAN KRAKEN'S BATHYSCAPHE!

!

?

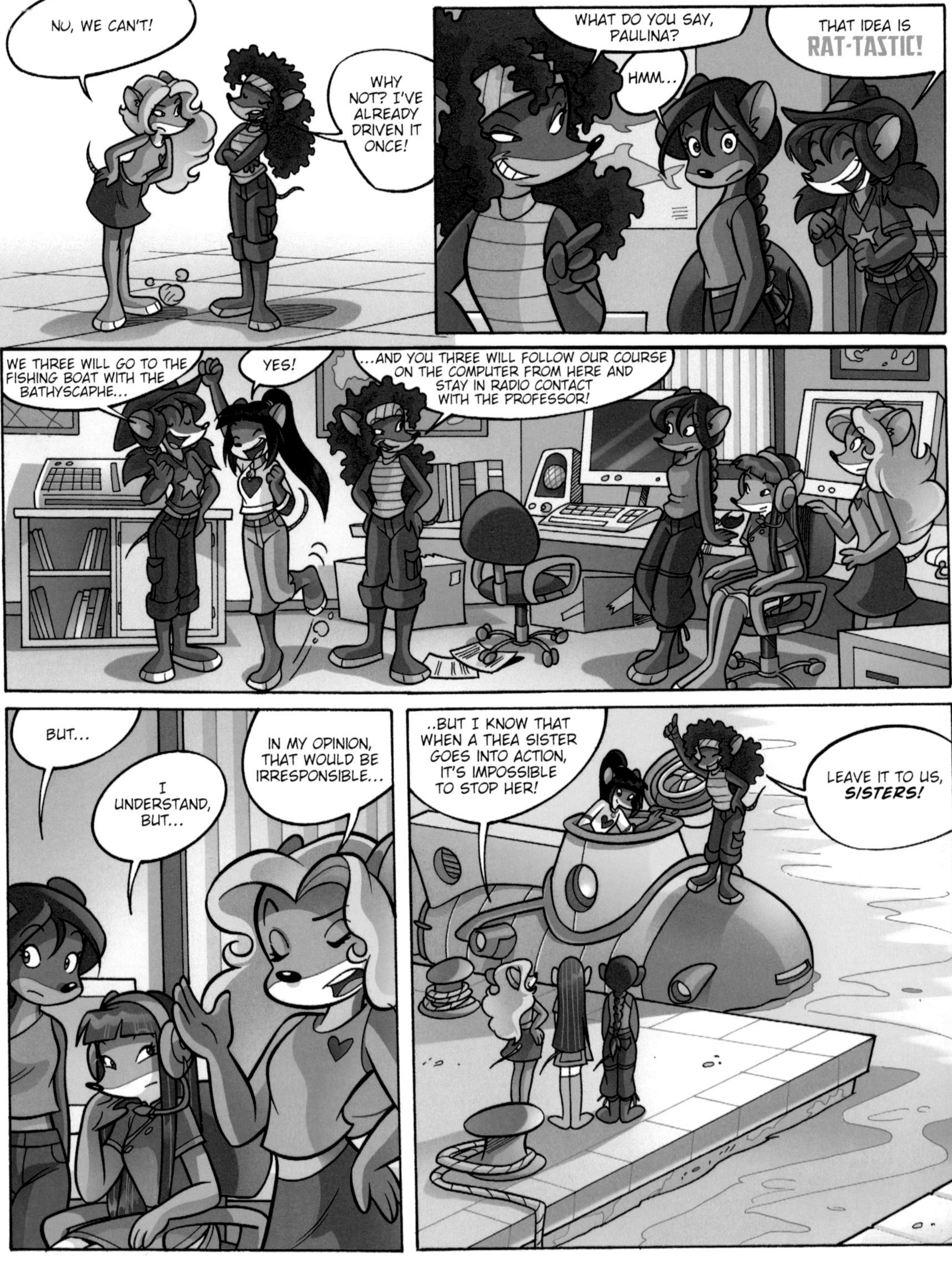
NO, WE CAN'T!
WHY NOT? I'VE ALREADY DRIVEN IT ONCE!
WHAT DO YOU SAY, PAULINA?
HMM...
THAT IDEA IS RAT-TASTIC!
WE THREE WILL GO TO THE FISHING BOAT WITH THE BATHYSCAPHE...
YES!
...AND YOU THREE WILL FOLLOW OUR COURSE ON THE COMPUTER FROM HERE AND STAY IN RADIO CONTACT WITH THE PROFESSOR!
BUT...
I UNDERSTAND, BUT...
IN MY OPINION, THAT WOULD BE IRRESPONSIBLE...
..BUT I KNOW THAT WHEN A THEA SISTER GOES INTO ACTION, IT'S IMPOSSIBLE TO STOP HER!
LEAVE IT TO US, SISTERS!

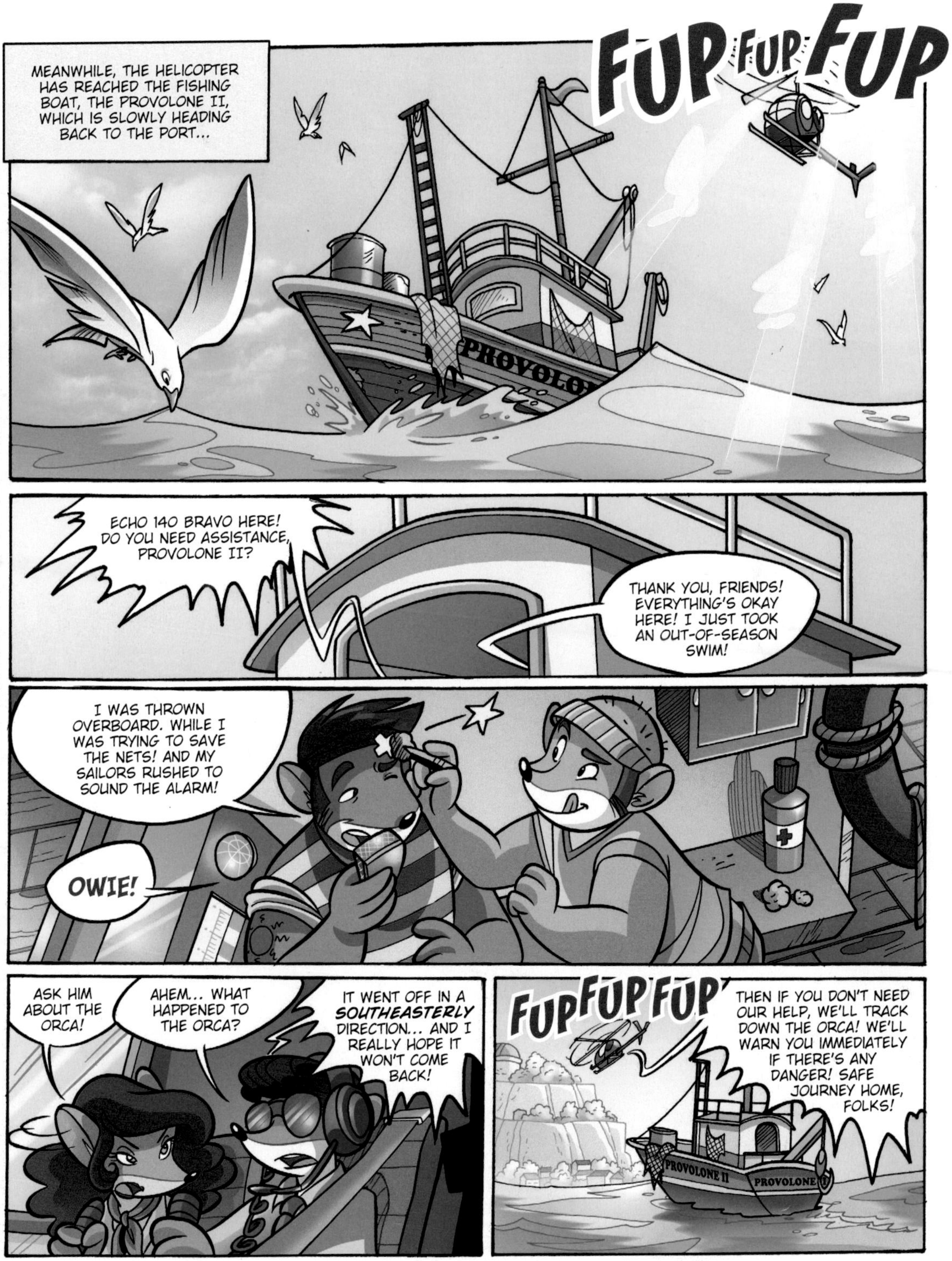
MEANWHILE, THE HELICOPTER HAS REACHED THE FISHING BOAT, THE PROVOLONE II, WHICH IS SLOWLY HEADING BACK TO THE PORT...
FUP FUP FUP
PROVOLONE
ECHO 140 BRAVO HERE! DO YOU NEED ASSISTANCE, PROVOLONE II?
THANK YOU, FRIENDS! EVERYTHING'S OKAY HERE! I JUST TOOK AN OUT-OF-SEASON SWIM!
I WAS THROWN OVERBOARD. WHILE I WAS TRYING TO SAVE THE NETS! AND MY SAILORS RUSHED TO SOUND THE ALARM!
OWIE!
ASK HIM ABOUT THE ORCA!
AHEM... WHAT HAPPENED TO THE ORCA?
IT WENT OFF IN A *SOUTHEASTERLY* DIRECTION... AND I REALLY HOPE IT WON'T COME BACK!
FUP FUP FUP
THEN IF YOU DON'T NEED OUR HELP, WE'LL TRACK DOWN THE ORCA! WE'LL WARN YOU IMMEDIATELY IF THERE'S ANY DANGER! SAFE JOURNEY HOME, FOLKS!
PROVOLONE II
PROVOLONE II

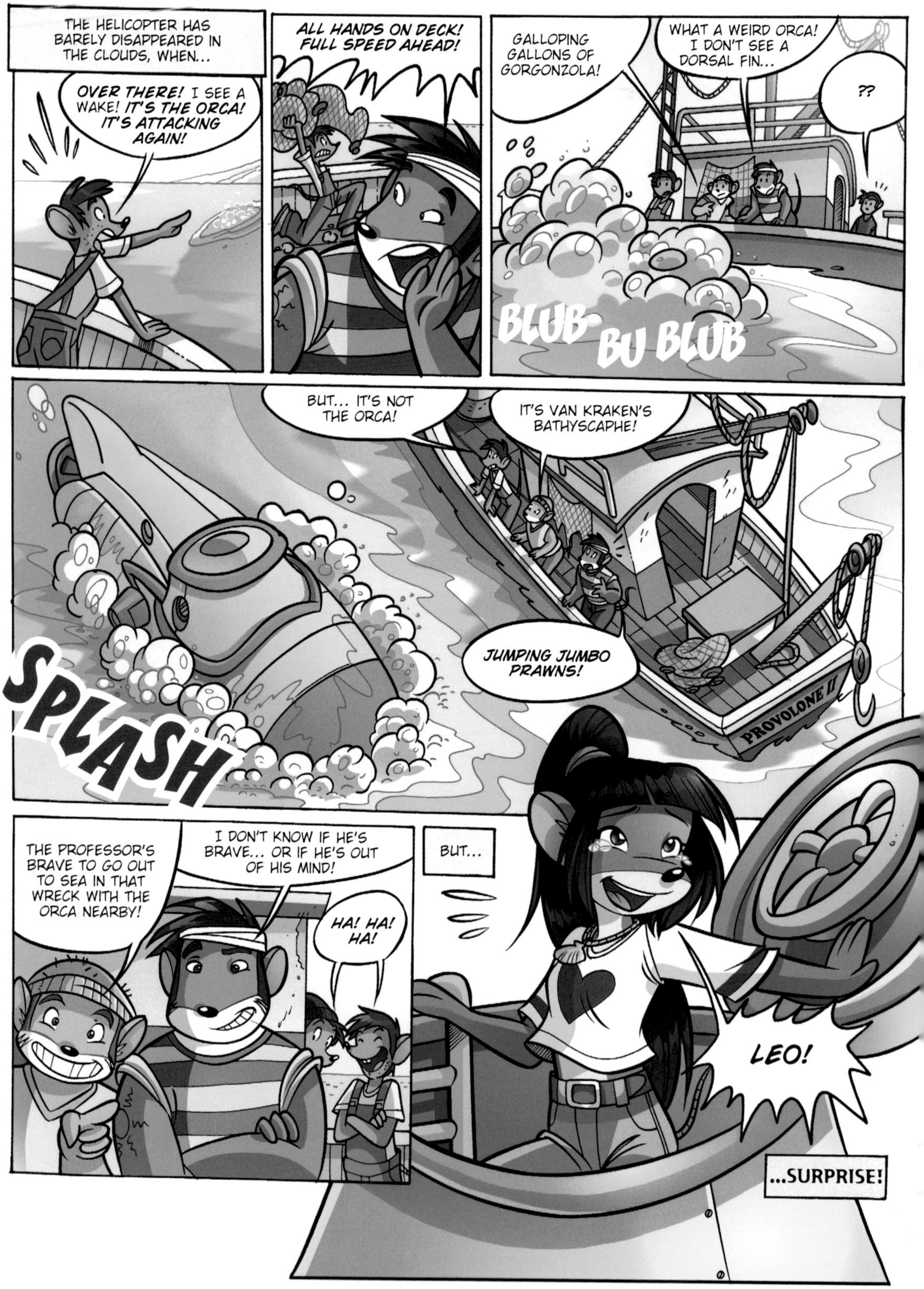
THE HELICOPTER HAS BARELY DISAPPEARED IN THE CLOUDS, WHEN...
OVER THERE! I SEE A WAKE! IT'S THE ORCA! IT'S ATTACKING AGAIN!
ALL HANDS ON DECK! FULL SPEED AHEAD!
GALLOPING GALLONS OF GORGONZOLA!
WHAT A WEIRD ORCA! I DON'T SEE A DORSAL FIN...
??
BLUB BU BLUB
BUT... IT'S NOT THE ORCA!
IT'S VAN KRAKEN'S BATHYSCAPHE!
JUMPING JUMBO PRAWNS!
SPLASH
PROVOLONE II
THE PROFESSOR'S BRAVE TO GO OUT TO SEA IN THAT WRECK WITH THE ORCA NEARBY!
I DON'T KNOW IF HE'S BRAVE... OR IF HE'S OUT OF HIS MIND!
HA! HA! HA!
BUT...
LEO!
...SURPRISE!

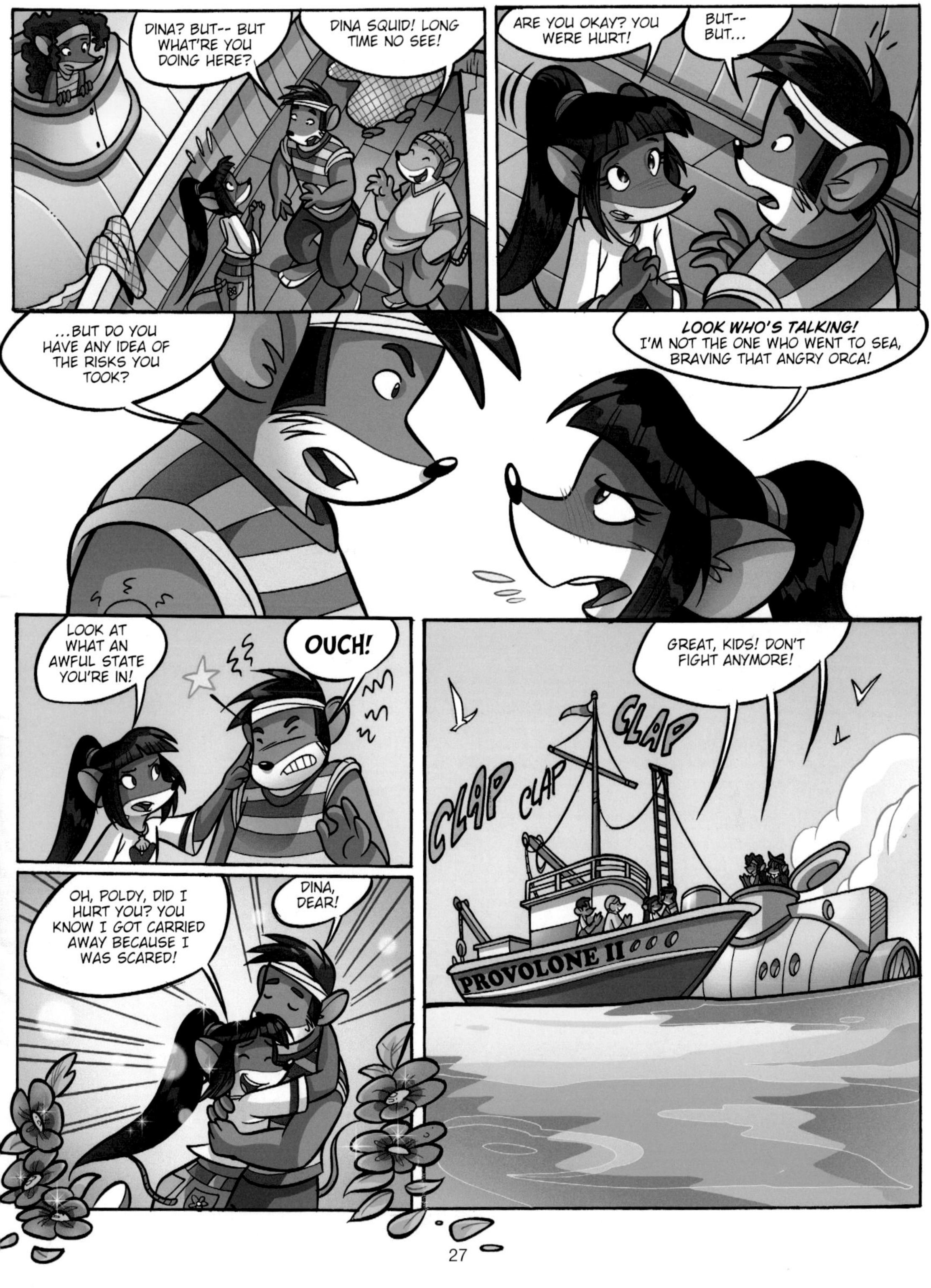
DINA? BUT-- BUT WHAT'RE YOU DOING HERE?
DINA SQUID! LONG TIME NO SEE!
ARE YOU OKAY? YOU WERE HURT!
BUT-- BUT...
...BUT DO YOU HAVE ANY IDEA OF THE RISKS YOU TOOK?
LOOK WHO'S TALKING! I'M NOT THE ONE WHO WENT TO SEA, BRAVING THAT ANGRY ORCA!
LOOK AT WHAT AN AWFUL STATE YOU'RE IN!
OUCH!
GREAT, KIDS! DON'T FIGHT ANYMORE!
CLAP
CLAP
CLAP
PROVOLONE II
OH, POLDY, DID I HURT YOU? YOU KNOW I GOT CARRIED AWAY BECAUSE I WAS SCARED!
DINA, DEAR!

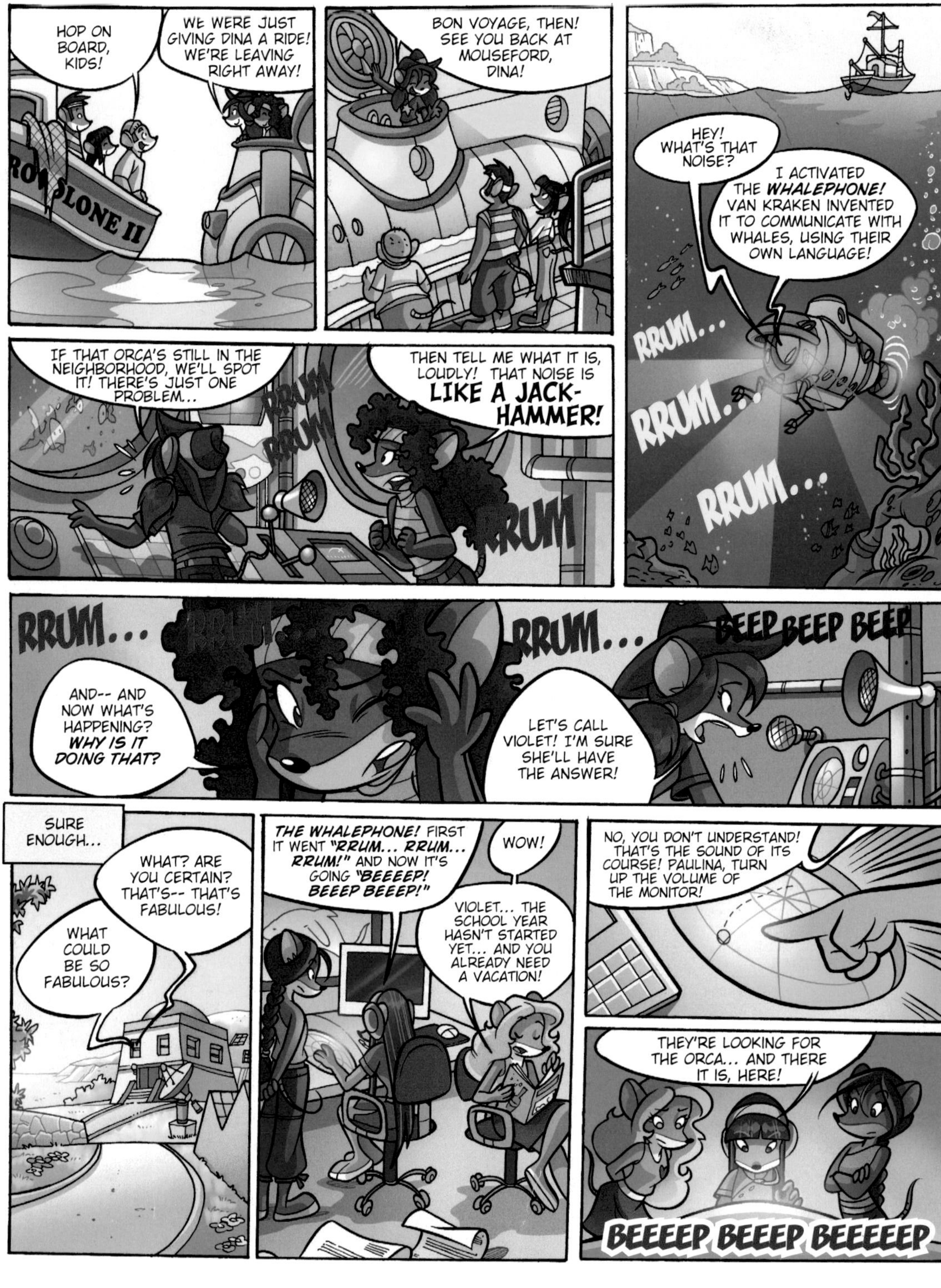
HOP ON BOARD, KIDS!
WE WERE JUST GIVING DINA A RIDE! WE'RE LEAVING RIGHT AWAY!
BON VOYAGE, THEN! SEE YOU BACK AT MOUSEFORD, DINA!
HEY! WHAT'S THAT NOISE?
I ACTIVATED THE WHALEPHONE! VAN KRAKEN INVENTED IT TO COMMUNICATE WITH WHALES, USING THEIR OWN LANGUAGE!
RRUM...
RRUM...
RRUM...
IF THAT ORCA'S STILL IN THE NEIGHBORHOOD, WE'LL SPOT IT! THERE'S JUST ONE PROBLEM...
THEN TELL ME WHAT IT IS, LOUDLY! THAT NOISE IS LIKE A JACK-HAMMER!
RRUM
RRUM
RRUM
RRUM...
RRUM...
BEEP BEEP BEEP
AND-- AND NOW WHAT'S HAPPENING? WHY IS IT DOING THAT?
LET'S CALL VIOLET! I'M SURE SHE'LL HAVE THE ANSWER!
SURE ENOUGH...
WHAT? ARE YOU CERTAIN? THAT'S-- THAT'S FABULOUS!
WHAT COULD BE SO FABULOUS?
THE WHALEPHONE! FIRST IT WENT "RRUM... RRUM... RRUM!" AND NOW IT'S GOING "BEEEEP! BEEEP BEEEP!"
WOW!
VIOLET... THE SCHOOL YEAR HASN'T STARTED YET... AND YOU ALREADY NEED A VACATION!
NO, YOU DON'T UNDERSTAND! THAT'S THE SOUND OF ITS COURSE! PAULINA, TURN UP THE VOLUME OF THE MONITOR!
THEY'RE LOOKING FOR THE ORCA... AND THERE IT IS, HERE!
BEEEEP BEEEP BEEEEEP

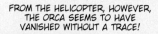

FROM THE HELICOPTER, HOWEVER, THE ORCA SEEMS TO HAVE VANISHED WITHOUT A TRACE!

NOTHING WE CAN DO! THERE'S NOT A TRACE OF THE ORCA...

FUP

FUP

FUP

FUP

THAT'S NOT POSSIBLE! IT CAN'T *DISAPPEAR* LIKE THAT!

HEY!

SWIPE

HA! HA! HA! WHAT'S POPPED INTO YOUR HEAD, PROFESSOR? I'M JUST WORRIED FOR THE POOR FISHERMEN WHO'RE THREATENED BY THAT **MONSTER!**

THAT *BEAST'S A TOUGH NUT TO CRACK!* BUT I CAN BE EVEN TOUGHER!

IT SOUNDS AS IF YOU HAVE A *SCORE TO SETTLE* WITH THE ORCA, MS. DE VISSEN!

THE ORCA ISN'T A MONSTER! THAT CREATURE IS A *SPLENDID SPECIMEN* AND VERY INTELLIGENT!

FUP FUP FUP FUP FUP

=TSK!= SO THEY SAY!

PROFESSOR! THERE'S A CERTAIN PAULINA ON THE RADIO FOR YOU! IT SOUNDS URGENT!

=GASP!= AND TO THINK THAT THIS WAS SUPPOSED TO BE A CALM DAY!

I HEAR YOU, PAULINA! WHAT'S HAPPENED?

NICKY AND PAMELA HAVE LOCATED THE ORCA, PROFESSOR!

FINALLY!

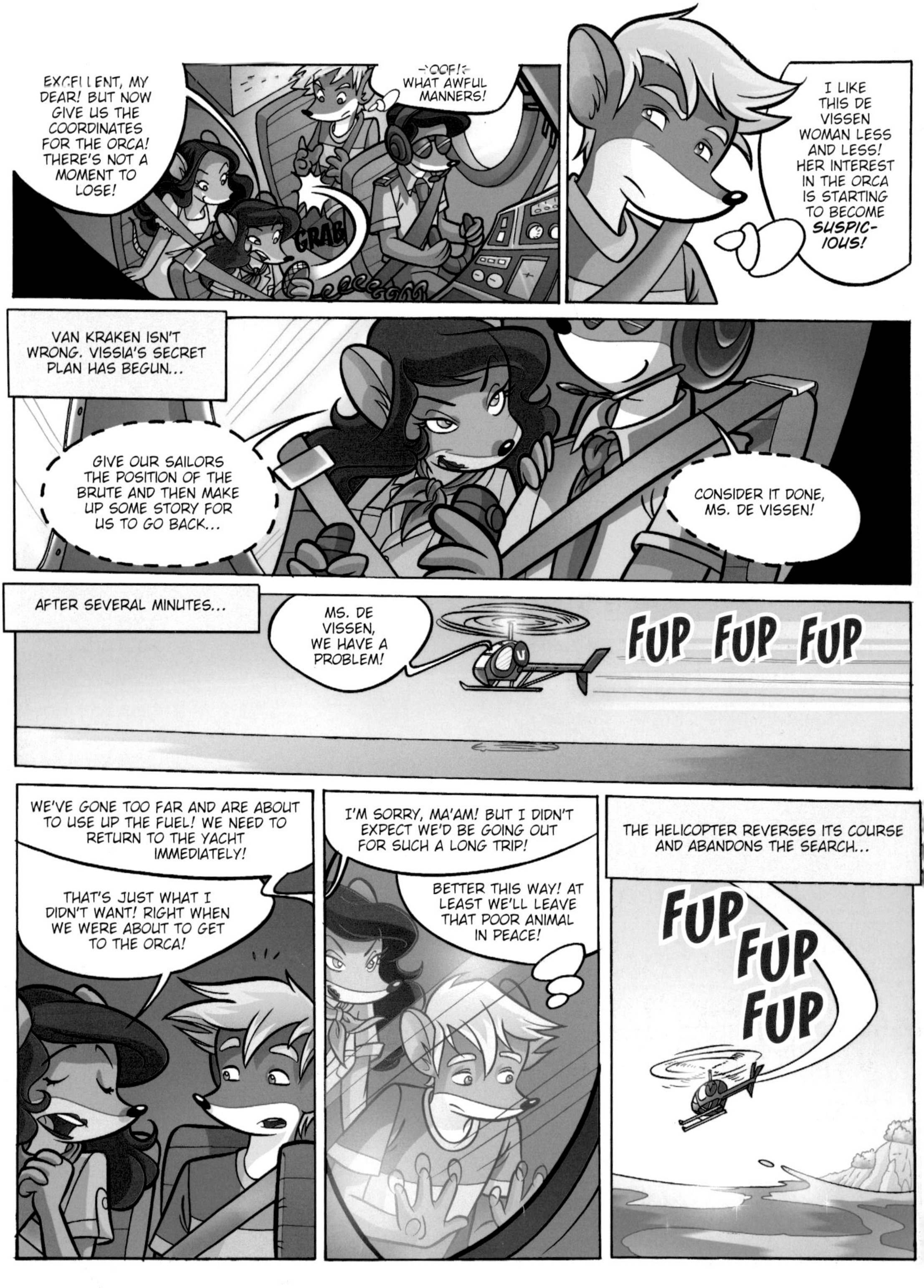

EXCELLENT, MY DEAR! BUT NOW GIVE US THE COORDINATES FOR THE ORCA! THERE'S NOT A MOMENT TO LOSE!
OOF! WHAT AWFUL MANNERS!
GRAB!
I LIKE THIS DE VISSEN WOMAN LESS AND LESS! HER INTEREST IN THE ORCA IS STARTING TO BECOME SUSPICIOUS!
VAN KRAKEN ISN'T WRONG. VISSIA'S SECRET PLAN HAS BEGUN...
GIVE OUR SAILORS THE POSITION OF THE BRUTE AND THEN MAKE UP SOME STORY FOR US TO GO BACK...
CONSIDER IT DONE, MS. DE VISSEN!
AFTER SEVERAL MINUTES...
MS. DE VISSEN, WE HAVE A PROBLEM!
FUP FUP FUP
WE'VE GONE TOO FAR AND ARE ABOUT TO USE UP THE FUEL! WE NEED TO RETURN TO THE YACHT IMMEDIATELY!
THAT'S JUST WHAT I DIDN'T WANT! RIGHT WHEN WE WERE ABOUT TO GET TO THE ORCA!
I'M SORRY, MA'AM! BUT I DIDN'T EXPECT WE'D BE GOING OUT FOR SUCH A LONG TRIP!
BETTER THIS WAY! AT LEAST WE'LL LEAVE THAT POOR ANIMAL IN PEACE!
THE HELICOPTER REVERSES ITS COURSE AND ABANDONS THE SEARCH...
FUP FUP FUP

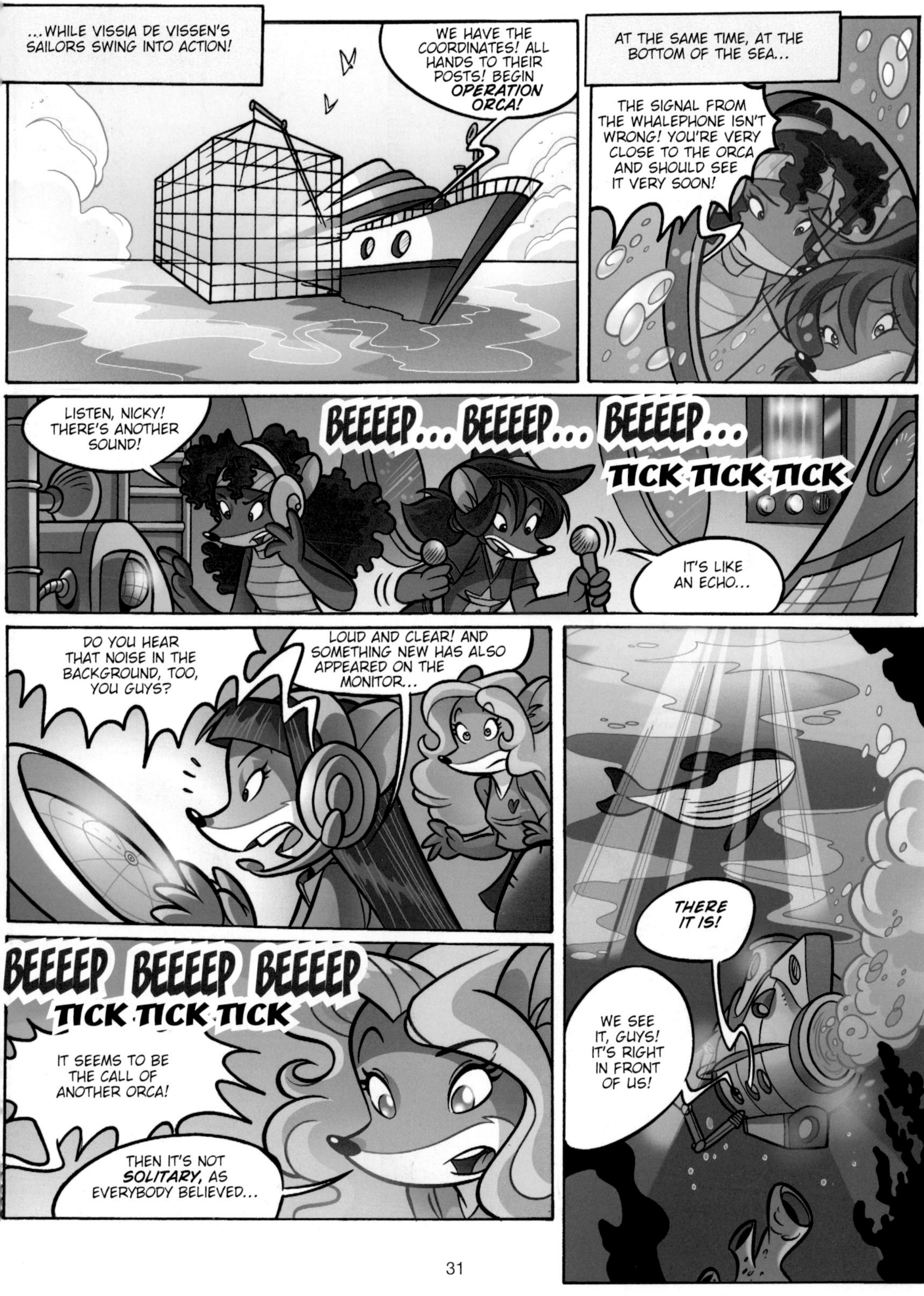
...WHILE VISSIA DE VISSEN'S SAILORS SWING INTO ACTION!
WE HAVE THE COORDINATES! ALL HANDS TO THEIR POSTS! BEGIN OPERATION ORCA!
AT THE SAME TIME, AT THE BOTTOM OF THE SEA...
THE SIGNAL FROM THE WHALEPHONE ISN'T WRONG! YOU'RE VERY CLOSE TO THE ORCA AND SHOULD SEE IT VERY SOON!
LISTEN, NICKY! THERE'S ANOTHER SOUND!
BEEEEP... BEEEEP... BEEEEP...
TICK TICK TICK
IT'S LIKE AN ECHO...
DO YOU HEAR THAT NOISE IN THE BACKGROUND, TOO, YOU GUYS?
LOUD AND CLEAR! AND SOMETHING NEW HAS ALSO APPEARED ON THE MONITOR...
BEEEEP BEEEEP BEEEEP
TICK TICK TICK
IT SEEMS TO BE THE CALL OF ANOTHER ORCA!
THEN IT'S NOT SOLITARY, AS EVERYBODY BELIEVED...
THERE IT IS!
WE SEE IT, GUYS! IT'S RIGHT IN FRONT OF US!

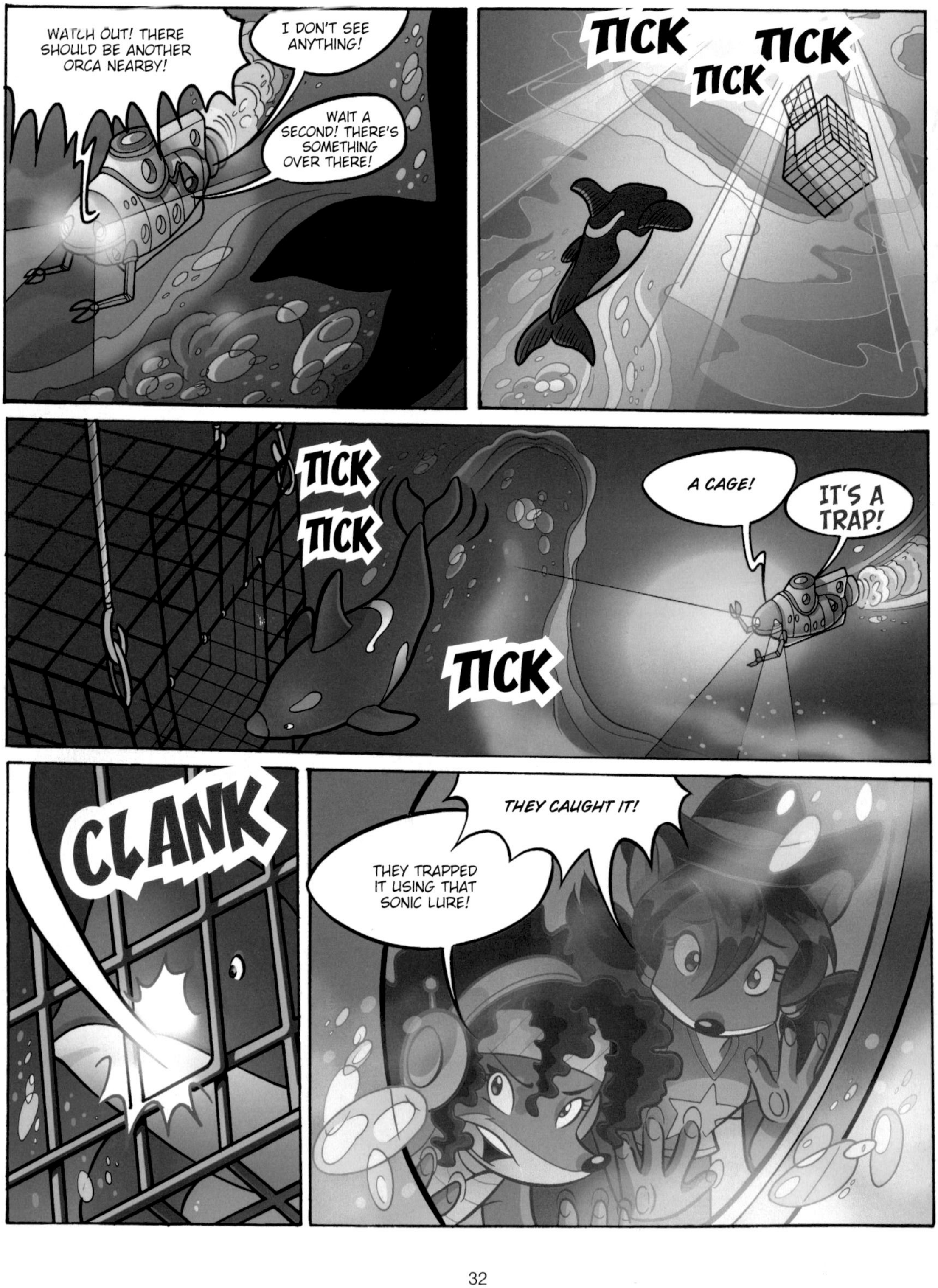

WATCH OUT! THERE SHOULD BE ANOTHER ORCA NEARBY!
I DON'T SEE ANYTHING!
WAIT A SECOND! THERE'S SOMETHING OVER THERE!
TICK
TICK
TICK
TICK
TICK
A CAGE!
IT'S A TRAP!
TICK
CLANK
THEY CAUGHT IT!
THEY TRAPPED IT USING THAT SONIC LURE!

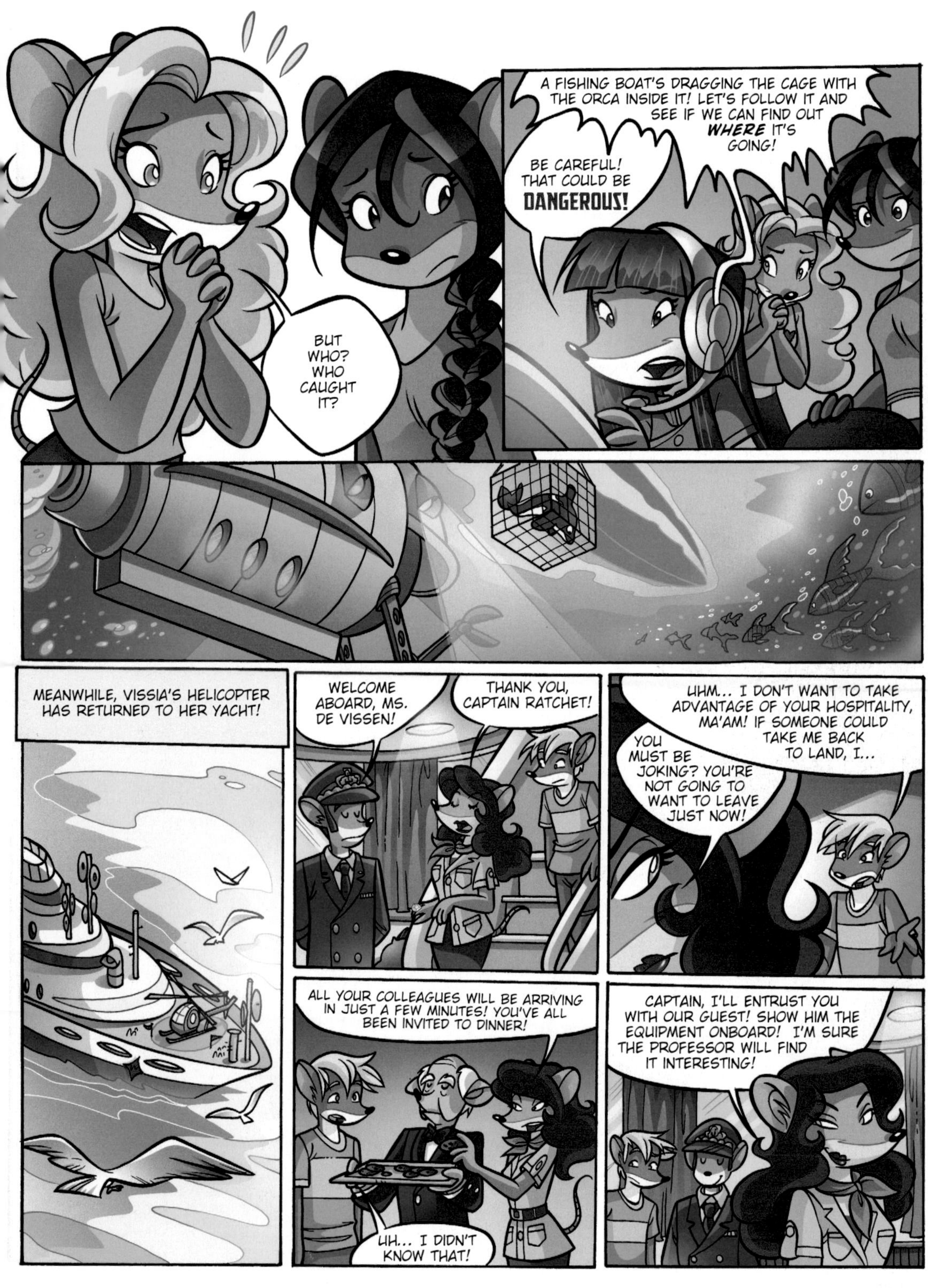
BUT WHO? WHO CAUGHT IT?
A FISHING BOAT'S DRAGGING THE CAGE WITH THE ORCA INSIDE IT! LET'S FOLLOW IT AND SEE IF WE CAN FIND OUT **WHERE** IT'S GOING!
BE CAREFUL! THAT COULD BE **DANGEROUS!**
MEANWHILE, VISSIA'S HELICOPTER HAS RETURNED TO HER YACHT!
WELCOME ABOARD, MS. DE VISSEN!
THANK YOU, CAPTAIN RATCHET!
UHM... I DON'T WANT TO TAKE ADVANTAGE OF YOUR HOSPITALITY, MA'AM! IF SOMEONE COULD TAKE ME BACK TO LAND, I...
YOU MUST BE JOKING? YOU'RE NOT GOING TO WANT TO LEAVE JUST NOW!
ALL YOUR COLLEAGUES WILL BE ARRIVING IN JUST A FEW MINUTES! YOU'VE ALL BEEN INVITED TO DINNER!
UH... I DIDN'T KNOW THAT!
CAPTAIN, I'LL ENTRUST YOU WITH OUR GUEST! SHOW HIM THE EQUIPMENT ONBOARD! I'M SURE THE PROFESSOR WILL FIND IT INTERESTING!

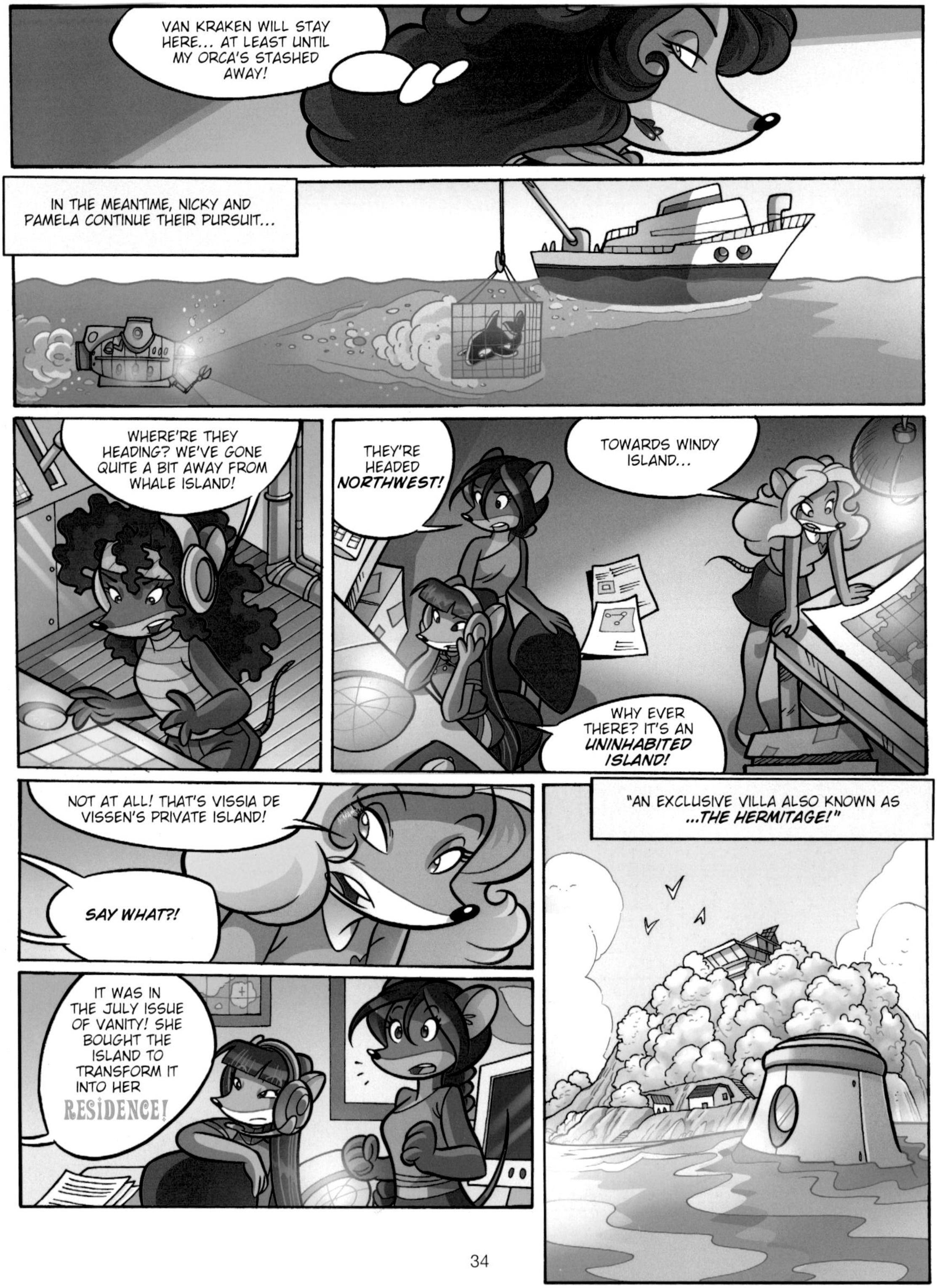

VAN KRAKEN WILL STAY HERE... AT LEAST UNTIL MY ORCA'S STASHED AWAY!
IN THE MEANTIME, NICKY AND PAMELA CONTINUE THEIR PURSUIT...
WHERE'RE THEY HEADING? WE'VE GONE QUITE A BIT AWAY FROM WHALE ISLAND!
THEY'RE HEADED **NORTHWEST!**
TOWARDS WINDY ISLAND...
WHY EVER THERE? IT'S AN ***UNINHABITED ISLAND!***
NOT AT ALL! THAT'S VISSIA DE VISSEN'S PRIVATE ISLAND!
SAY WHAT?!
IT WAS IN THE JULY ISSUE OF VANITY! SHE BOUGHT THE ISLAND TO TRANSFORM IT INTO HER RESIDENCE!
"AN EXCLUSIVE VILLA ALSO KNOWN AS ***...THE HERMITAGE!***"

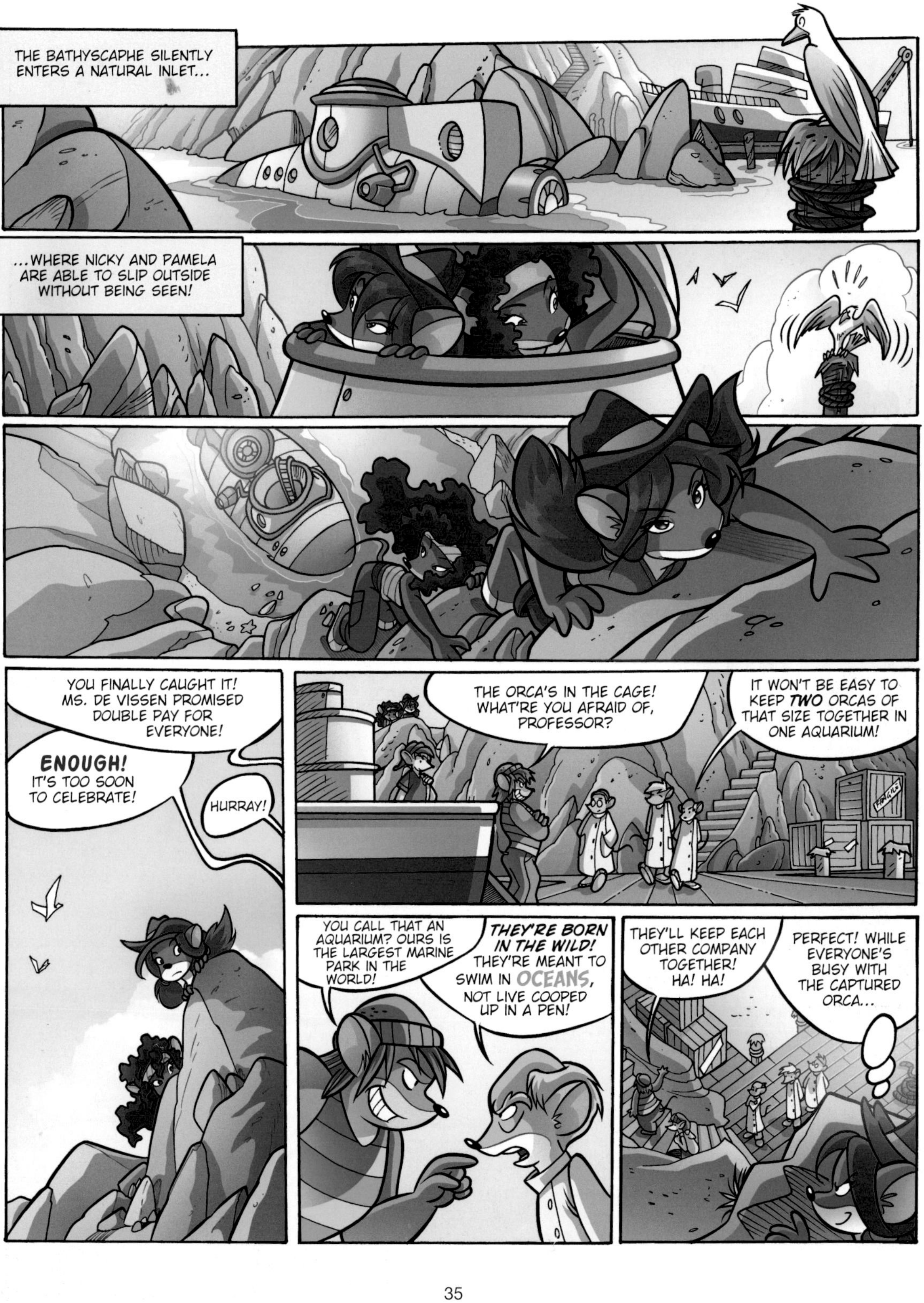
THE BATHYSCAPHE SILENTLY ENTERS A NATURAL INLET...
...WHERE NICKY AND PAMELA ARE ABLE TO SLIP OUTSIDE WITHOUT BEING SEEN!
YOU FINALLY CAUGHT IT! MS. DE VISSEN PROMISED DOUBLE PAY FOR EVERYONE!
ENOUGH! IT'S TOO SOON TO CELEBRATE!
HURRAY!
THE ORCA'S IN THE CAGE! WHAT'RE YOU AFRAID OF, PROFESSOR?
IT WON'T BE EASY TO KEEP TWO ORCAS OF THAT SIZE TOGETHER IN ONE AQUARIUM!
FRAGILE
YOU CALL THAT AN AQUARIUM? OURS IS THE LARGEST MARINE PARK IN THE WORLD!
THEY'RE BORN IN THE WILD! THEY'RE MEANT TO SWIM IN OCEANS, NOT LIVE COOPED UP IN A PEN!
THEY'LL KEEP EACH OTHER COMPANY TOGETHER! HA! HA!
PERFECT! WHILE EVERYONE'S BUSY WITH THE CAPTURED ORCA...

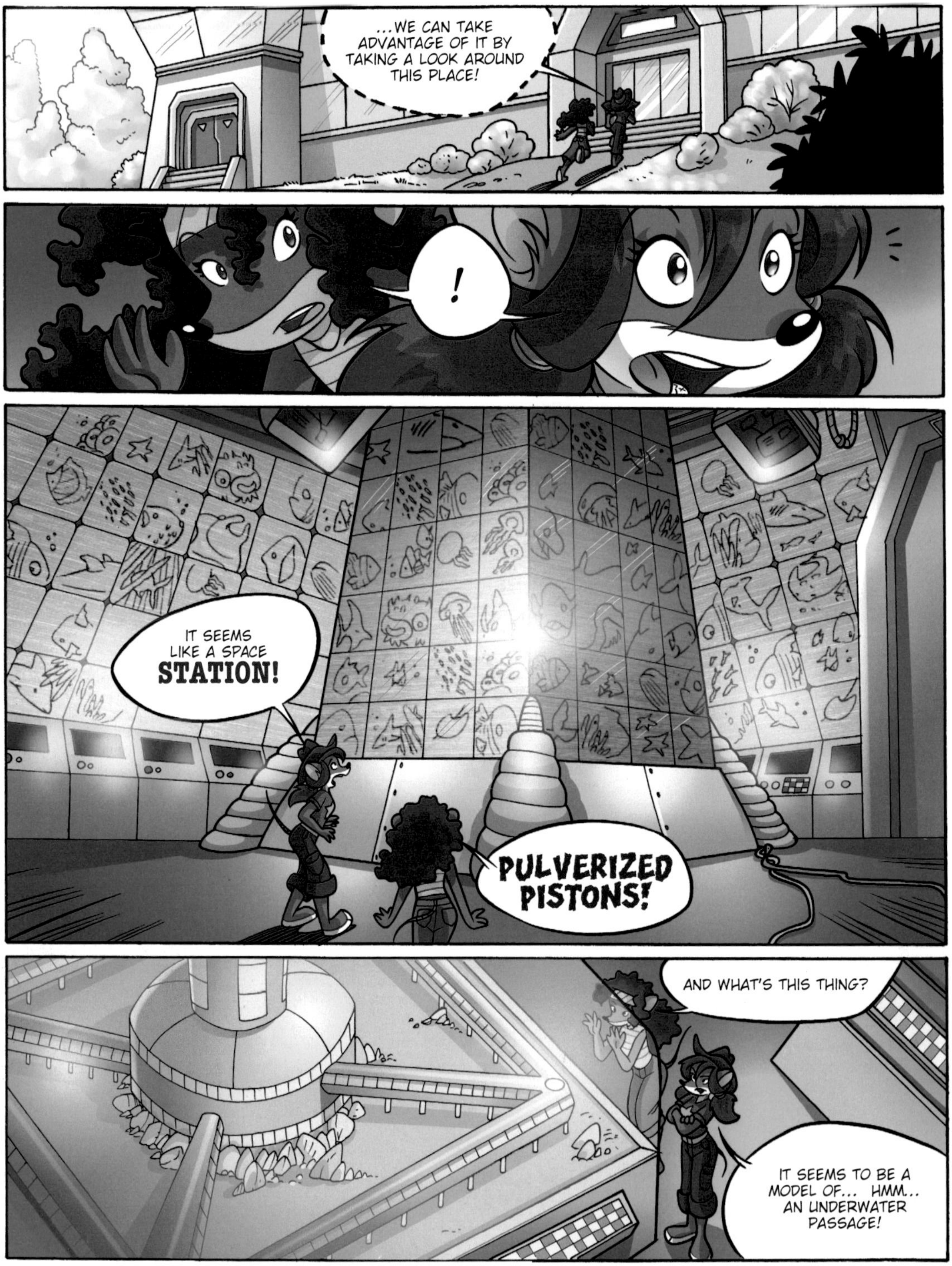
...WE CAN TAKE ADVANTAGE OF IT BY TAKING A LOOK AROUND THIS PLACE!
!
IT SEEMS LIKE A SPACE STATION!
PULVERIZED PISTONS!
AND WHAT'S THIS THING?
IT SEEMS TO BE A MODEL OF... HMM... AN UNDERWATER PASSAGE!

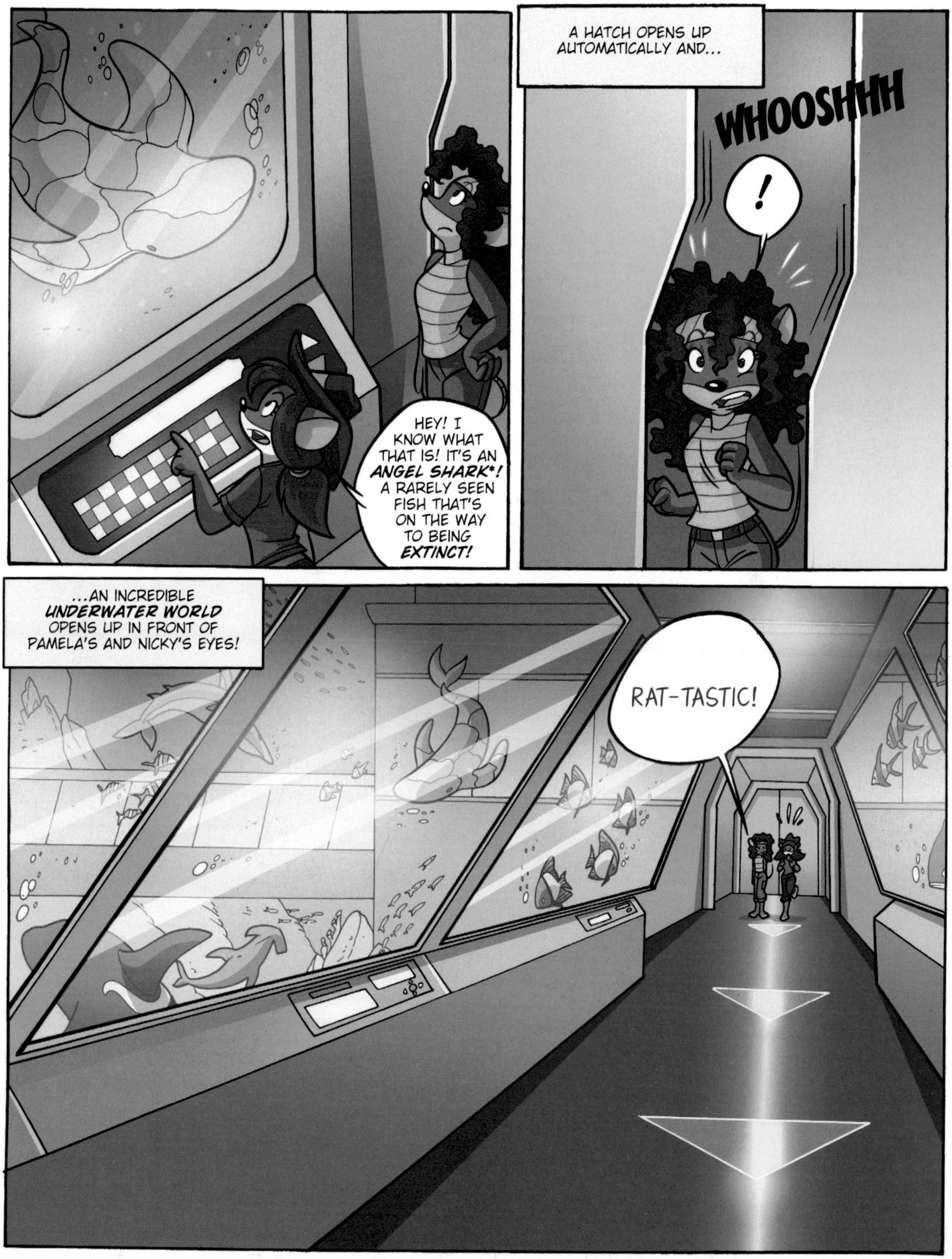
HEY! I KNOW WHAT THAT IS! IT'S AN ***ANGEL SHARK****! A RARELY SEEN FISH THAT'S ON THE WAY TO BEING ***EXTINCT!***
A HATCH OPENS UP AUTOMATICALLY AND...
WHOOSHHH
!
...AN INCREDIBLE ***UNDERWATER WORLD*** OPENS UP IN FRONT OF PAMELA'S AND NICKY'S EYES!
RAT-TASTIC!

* THE TWO WINGS OF THE ANGEL SHARK ARE ACTUALLY ITS PECTORAL FINS. IT LIVES ALONG THE COASTS IN TEMPERATE WATERS. DURING THE DAY IT SPENDS ITS TIME HIDDEN UNDER THE SAND, LEAVING ONLY ITS EYES SHOWING.

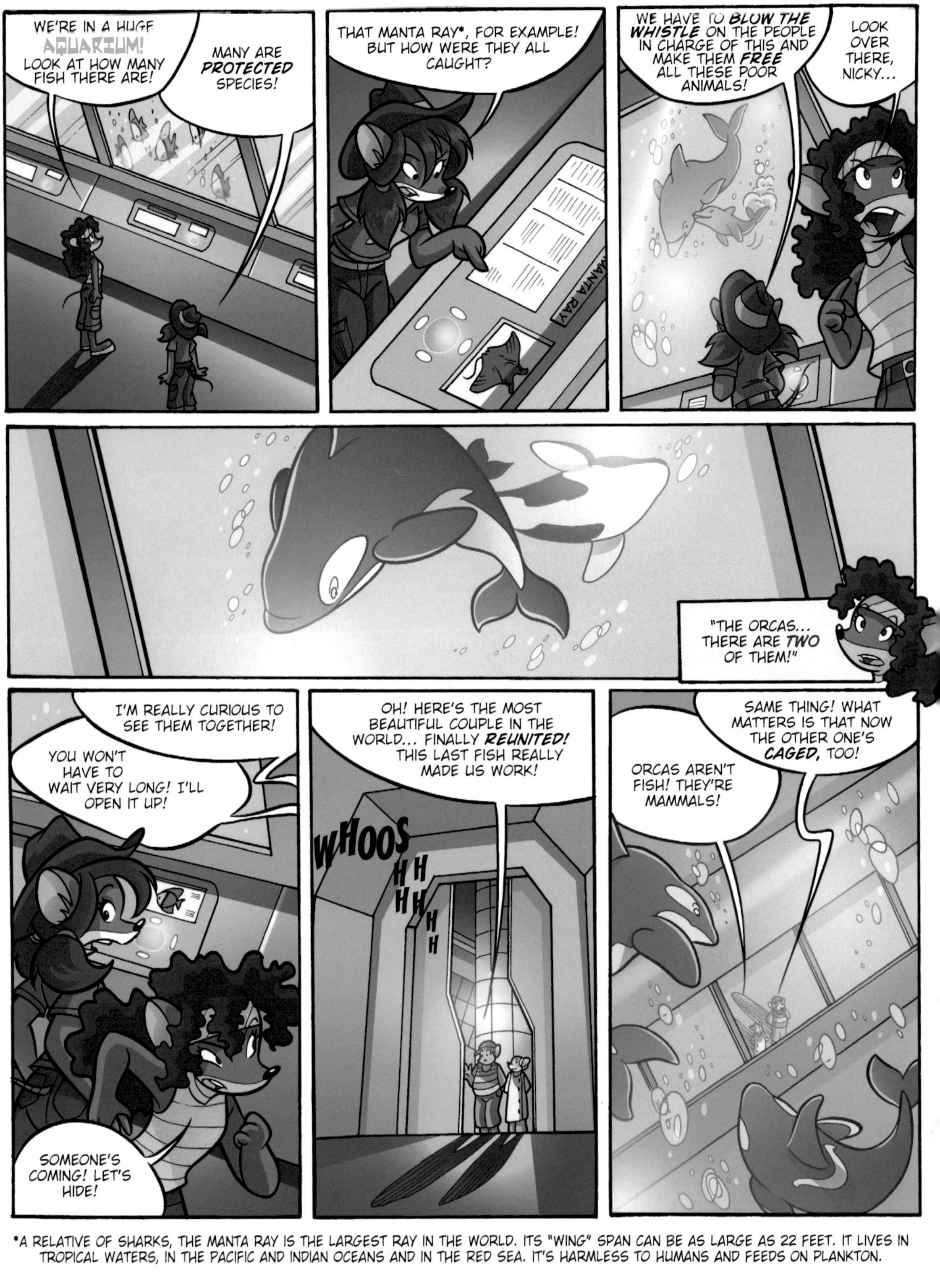
WE'RE IN A HUGE AQUARIUM! LOOK AT HOW MANY FISH THERE ARE!
MANY ARE PROTECTED SPECIES!
THAT MANTA RAY*, FOR EXAMPLE! BUT HOW WERE THEY ALL CAUGHT?
MANTA RAY
WE HAVE TO BLOW THE WHISTLE ON THE PEOPLE IN CHARGE OF THIS AND MAKE THEM FREE ALL THESE POOR ANIMALS!
LOOK OVER THERE, NICKY...
"THE ORCAS... THERE ARE TWO OF THEM!"
I'M REALLY CURIOUS TO SEE THEM TOGETHER!
YOU WON'T HAVE TO WAIT VERY LONG! I'LL OPEN IT UP!
SOMEONE'S COMING! LET'S HIDE!
OH! HERE'S THE MOST BEAUTIFUL COUPLE IN THE WORLD... FINALLY REUNITED! THIS LAST FISH REALLY MADE US WORK!
WHOOSHHHHHH
SAME THING! WHAT MATTERS IS THAT NOW THE OTHER ONE'S CAGED, TOO!
ORCAS AREN'T FISH! THEY'RE MAMMALS!

*A RELATIVE OF SHARKS, THE MANTA RAY IS THE LARGEST RAY IN THE WORLD. ITS "WING" SPAN CAN BE AS LARGE AS 22 FEET. IT LIVES IN TROPICAL WATERS, IN THE PACIFIC AND INDIAN OCEANS AND IN THE RED SEA. IT'S HARMLESS TO HUMANS AND FEEDS ON PLANKTON.

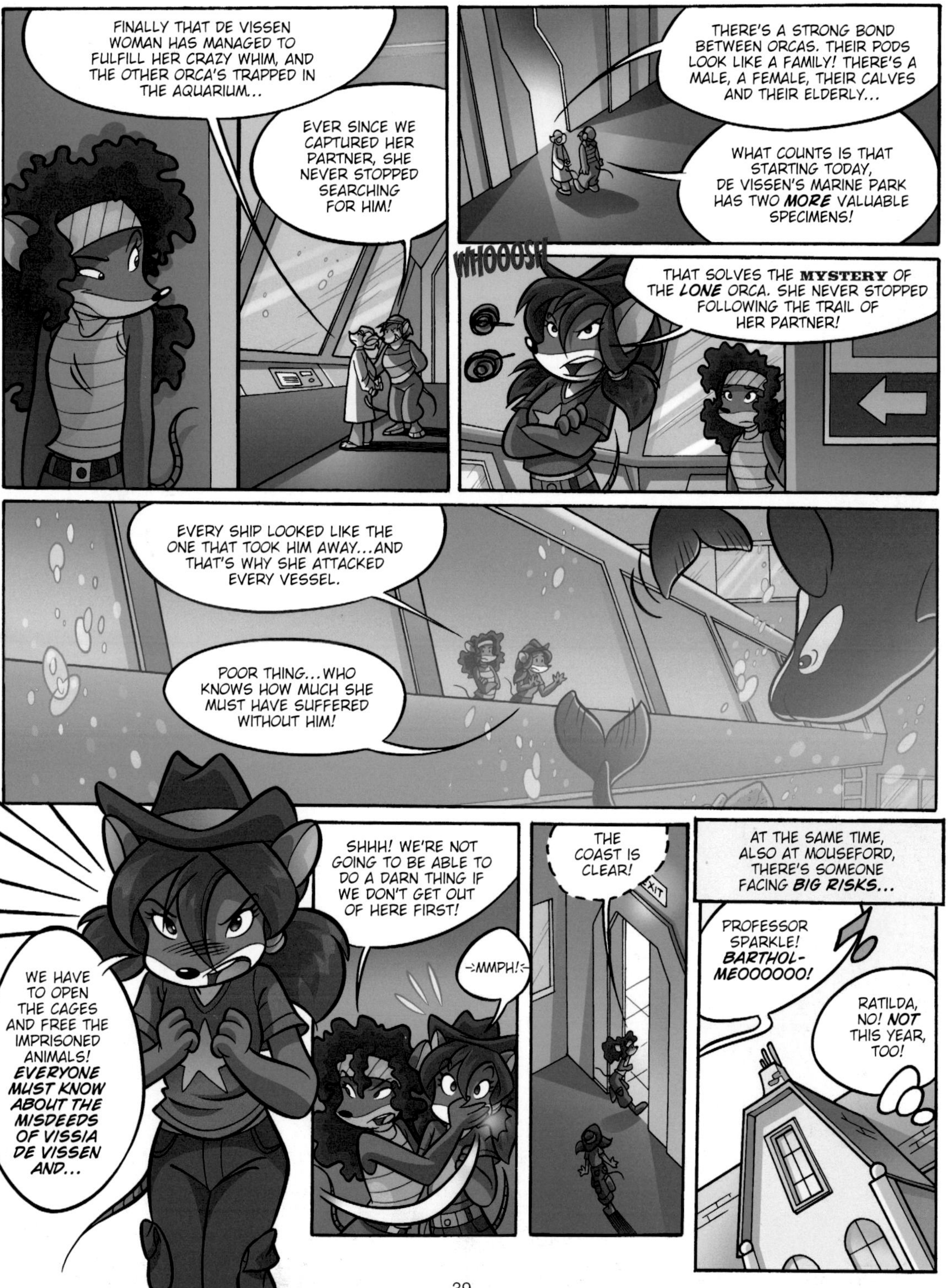
FINALLY THAT DE VISSEN WOMAN HAS MANAGED TO FULFILL HER CRAZY WHIM, AND THE OTHER ORCA'S TRAPPED IN THE AQUARIUM...
EVER SINCE WE CAPTURED HER PARTNER, SHE NEVER STOPPED SEARCHING FOR HIM!
THERE'S A STRONG BOND BETWEEN ORCAS. THEIR PODS LOOK LIKE A FAMILY! THERE'S A MALE, A FEMALE, THEIR CALVES AND THEIR ELDERLY...
WHAT COUNTS IS THAT STARTING TODAY, DE VISSEN'S MARINE PARK HAS TWO MORE VALUABLE SPECIMENS!
WHOOOSH
THAT SOLVES THE MYSTERY OF THE LONE ORCA. SHE NEVER STOPPED FOLLOWING THE TRAIL OF HER PARTNER!
EVERY SHIP LOOKED LIKE THE ONE THAT TOOK HIM AWAY...AND THAT'S WHY SHE ATTACKED EVERY VESSEL.
POOR THING...WHO KNOWS HOW MUCH SHE MUST HAVE SUFFERED WITHOUT HIM!
WE HAVE TO OPEN THE CAGES AND FREE THE IMPRISONED ANIMALS! EVERYONE MUST KNOW ABOUT THE MISDEEDS OF VISSIA DE VISSEN AND...
SHHH! WE'RE NOT GOING TO BE ABLE TO DO A DARN THING IF WE DON'T GET OUT OF HERE FIRST!
MMPH!
THE COAST IS CLEAR!
EXIT
AT THE SAME TIME, ALSO AT MOUSEFORD, THERE'S SOMEONE FACING BIG RISKS...
PROFESSOR SPARKLE! BARTHOL-MEOOOOOO!
RATILDA, NO! NOT THIS YEAR, TOO!

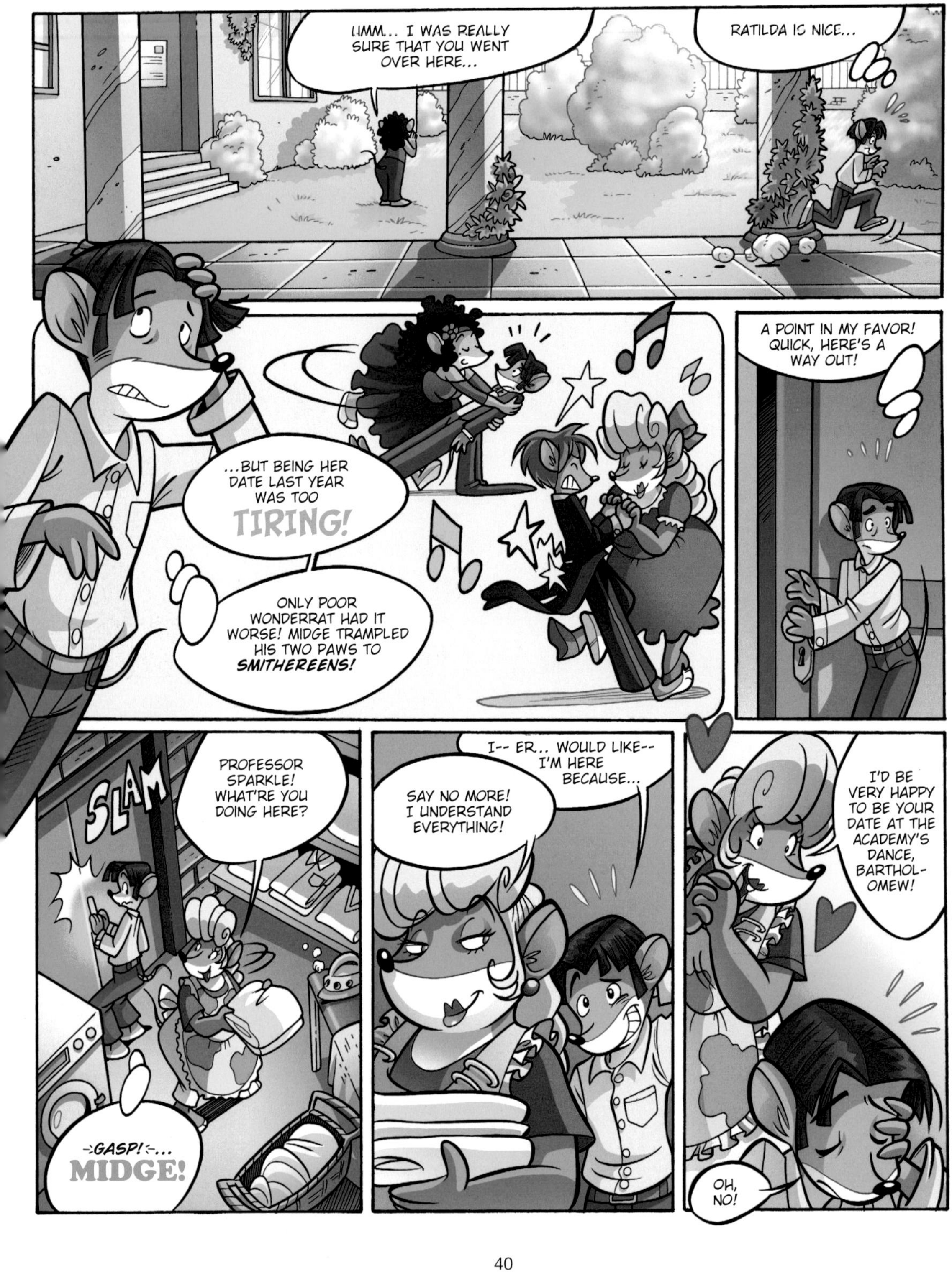
UMM... I WAS REALLY SURE THAT YOU WENT OVER HERE...
RATILDA IS NICE...
...BUT BEING HER DATE LAST YEAR WAS TOO TIRING!
ONLY POOR WONDERRAT HAD IT WORSE! MIDGE TRAMPLED HIS TWO PAWS TO SMITHEREENS!
A POINT IN MY FAVOR! QUICK, HERE'S A WAY OUT!
SLAM
PROFESSOR SPARKLE! WHAT'RE YOU DOING HERE?
GASP!... MIDGE!
I-- ER... WOULD LIKE-- I'M HERE BECAUSE...
SAY NO MORE! I UNDERSTAND EVERYTHING!
I'D BE VERY HAPPY TO BE YOUR DATE AT THE ACADEMY'S DANCE, BARTHOLOMEW!
OH, NO!

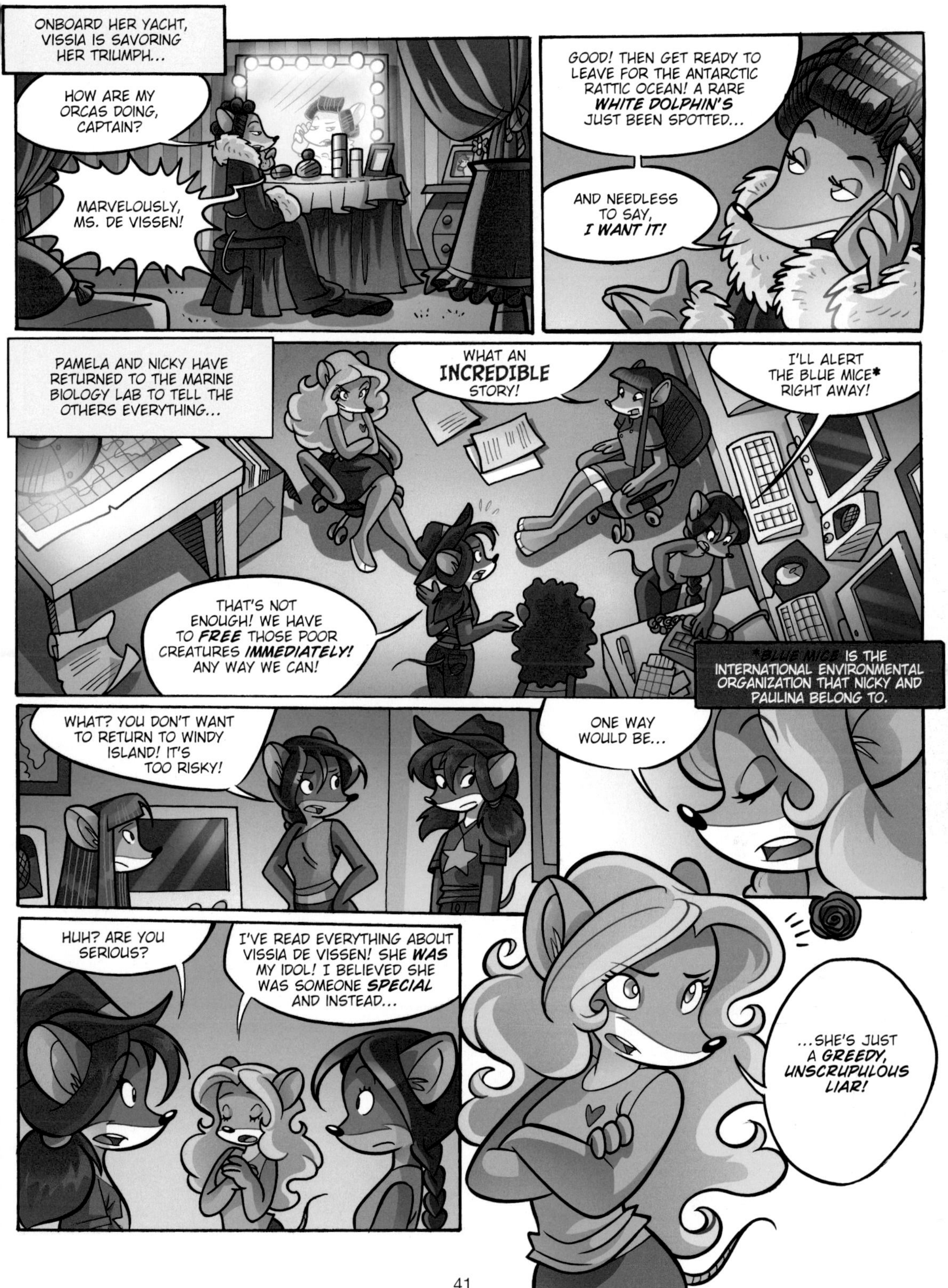
ONBOARD HER YACHT, VISSIA IS SAVORING HER TRIUMPH...
HOW ARE MY ORCAS DOING, CAPTAIN?
MARVELOUSLY, MS. DE VISSEN!
GOOD! THEN GET READY TO LEAVE FOR THE ANTARCTIC RATTIC OCEAN! A RARE WHITE DOLPHIN'S JUST BEEN SPOTTED...
AND NEEDLESS TO SAY, I WANT IT!
PAMELA AND NICKY HAVE RETURNED TO THE MARINE BIOLOGY LAB TO TELL THE OTHERS EVERYTHING...
WHAT AN INCREDIBLE STORY!
I'LL ALERT THE BLUE MICE* RIGHT AWAY!
THAT'S NOT ENOUGH! WE HAVE TO FREE THOSE POOR CREATURES IMMEDIATELY! ANY WAY WE CAN!
*BLUE MICE IS THE INTERNATIONAL ENVIRONMENTAL ORGANIZATION THAT NICKY AND PAULINA BELONG TO.
WHAT? YOU DON'T WANT TO RETURN TO WINDY ISLAND! IT'S TOO RISKY!
ONE WAY WOULD BE...
HUH? ARE YOU SERIOUS?
I'VE READ EVERYTHING ABOUT VISSIA DE VISSEN! SHE WAS MY IDOL! I BELIEVED SHE WAS SOMEONE SPECIAL AND INSTEAD...
...SHE'S JUST A GREEDY, UNSCRUPULOUS LIAR!

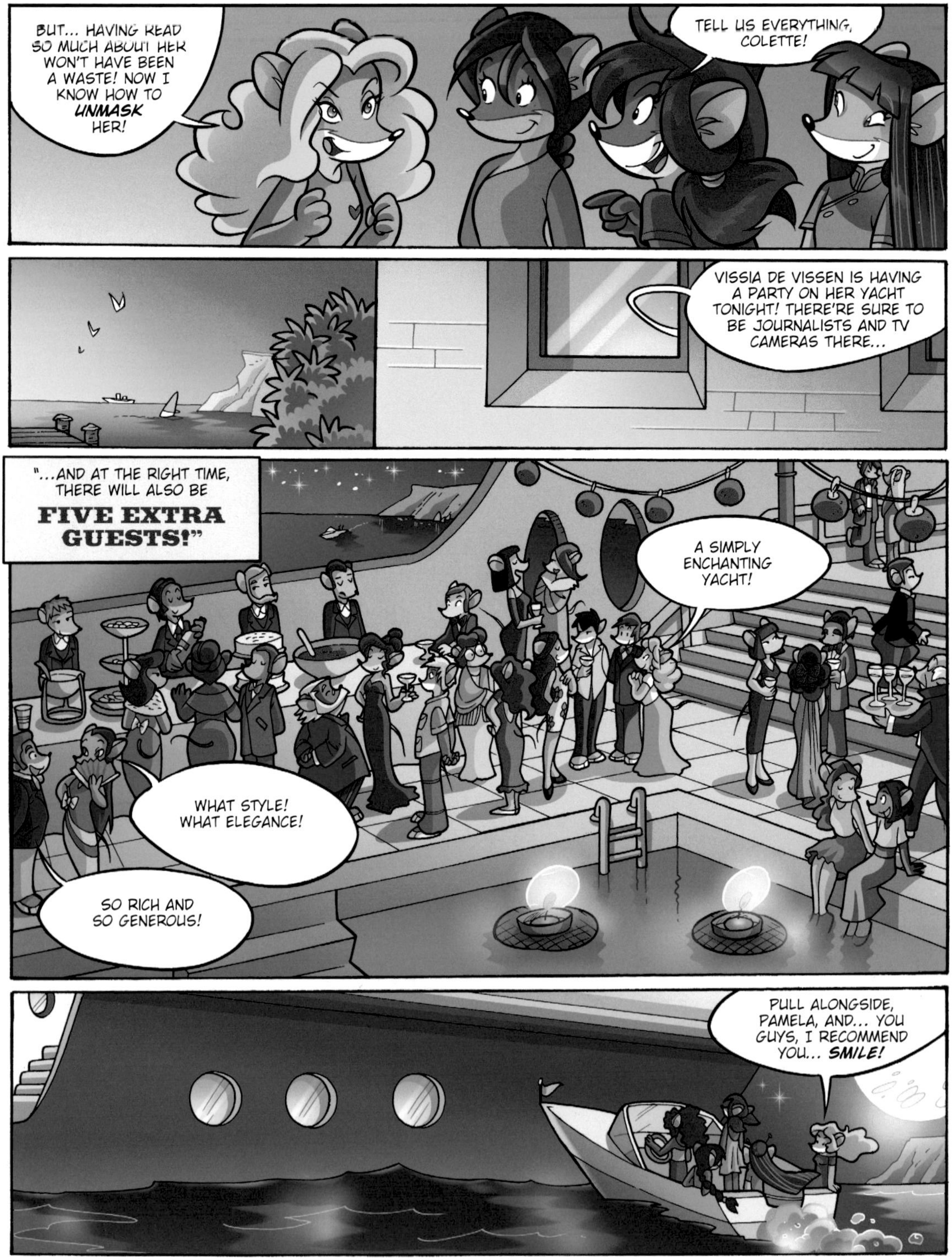
BUT... HAVING READ SO MUCH ABOUT HER WON'T HAVE BEEN A WASTE! NOW I KNOW HOW TO UNMASK HER!
TELL US EVERYTHING, COLETTE!
VISSIA DE VISSEN IS HAVING A PARTY ON HER YACHT TONIGHT! THERE'RE SURE TO BE JOURNALISTS AND TV CAMERAS THERE...
"...AND AT THE RIGHT TIME, THERE WILL ALSO BE FIVE EXTRA GUESTS!"
A SIMPLY ENCHANTING YACHT!
WHAT STYLE! WHAT ELEGANCE!
SO RICH AND SO GENEROUS!
PULL ALONGSIDE, PAMELA, AND... YOU GUYS, I RECOMMEND YOU... SMILE!

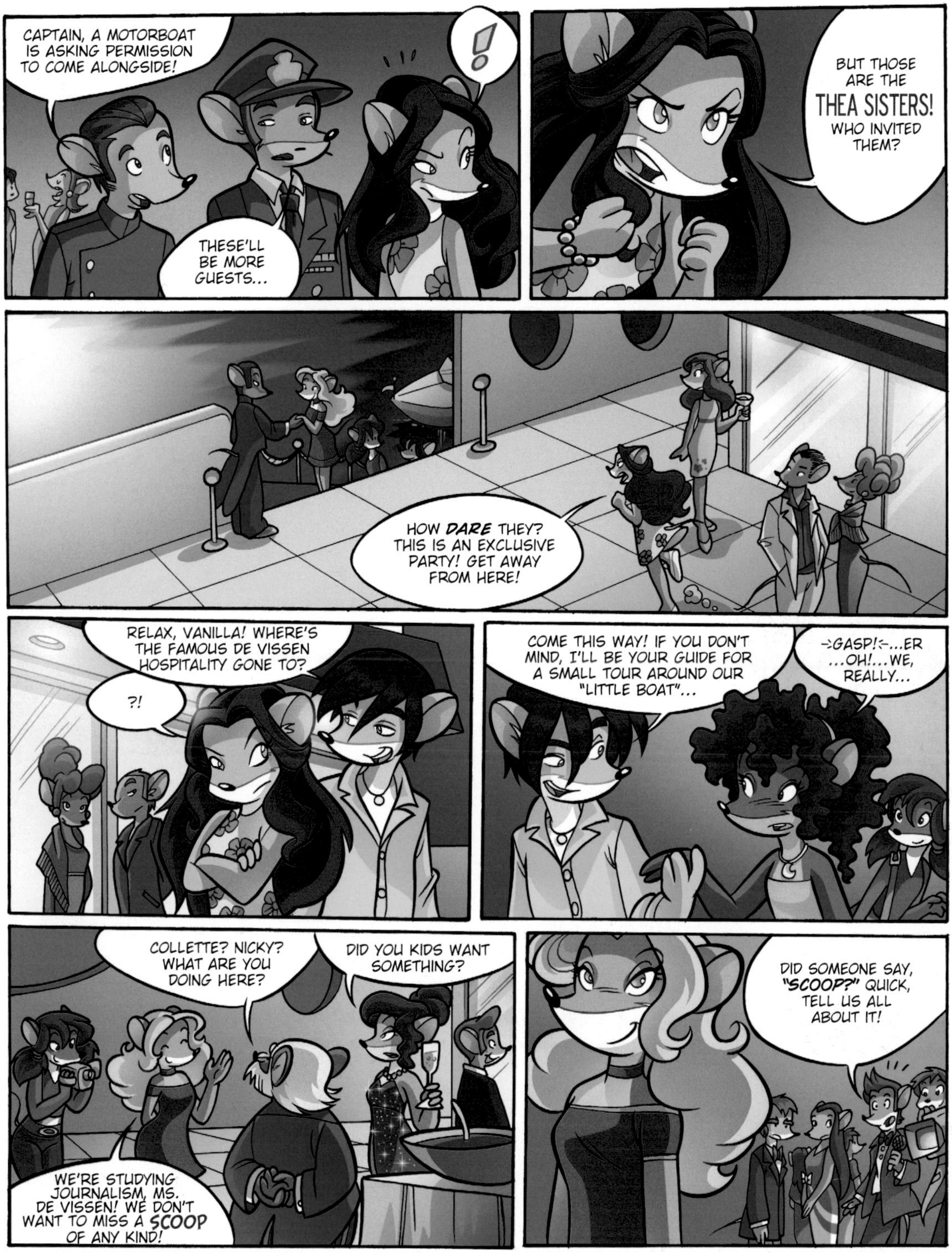
CAPTAIN, A MOTORBOAT IS ASKING PERMISSION TO COME ALONGSIDE!
!
THESE'LL BE MORE GUESTS...
BUT THOSE ARE THE THEA SISTERS! WHO INVITED THEM?
HOW DARE THEY? THIS IS AN EXCLUSIVE PARTY! GET AWAY FROM HERE!
RELAX, VANILLA! WHERE'S THE FAMOUS DE VISSEN HOSPITALITY GONE TO?
?!
COME THIS WAY! IF YOU DON'T MIND, I'LL BE YOUR GUIDE FOR A SMALL TOUR AROUND OUR "LITTLE BOAT"...
→GASP!←...ER ...OH!...WE, REALLY...
COLLETTE? NICKY? WHAT ARE YOU DOING HERE?
DID YOU KIDS WANT SOMETHING?
WE'RE STUDYING JOURNALISM, MS. DE VISSEN! WE DON'T WANT TO MISS A SCOOP OF ANY KIND!
DID SOMEONE SAY, "SCOOP?" QUICK, TELL US ALL ABOUT IT!

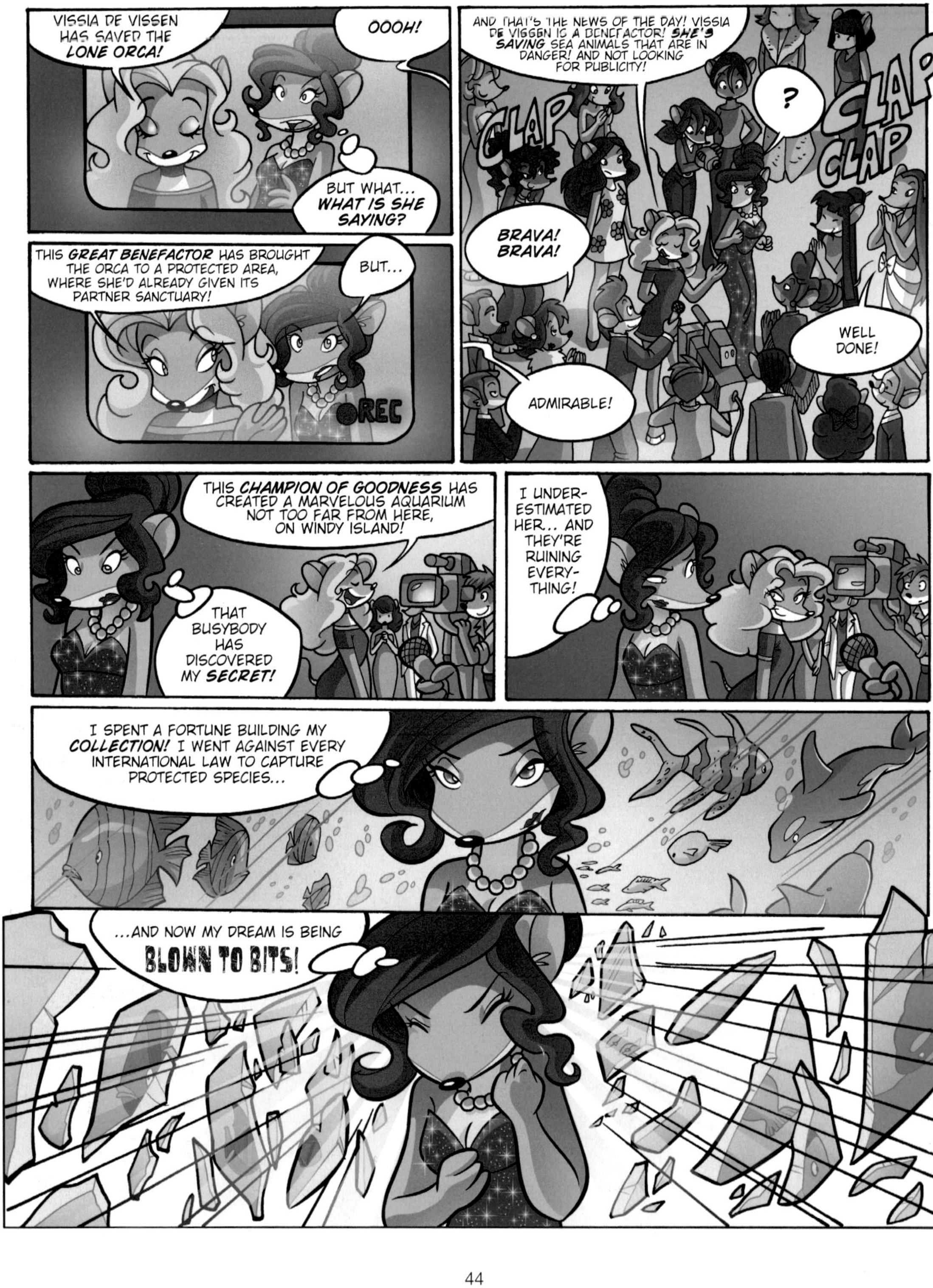
VISSIA DE VISSEN HAS SAVED THE LONE ORCA!
OOOH!
BUT WHAT... WHAT IS SHE SAYING?
AND THAT'S THE NEWS OF THE DAY! VISSIA DE VISSEN IS A BENEFACTOR! SHE'S SAVING SEA ANIMALS THAT ARE IN DANGER! AND NOT LOOKING FOR PUBLICITY!
?
CLAP
CLAP
CLAP
BRAVA! BRAVA!
THIS GREAT BENEFACTOR HAS BROUGHT THE ORCA TO A PROTECTED AREA, WHERE SHE'D ALREADY GIVEN ITS PARTNER SANCTUARY!
BUT...
REC
WELL DONE!
ADMIRABLE!
THIS CHAMPION OF GOODNESS HAS CREATED A MARVELOUS AQUARIUM NOT TOO FAR FROM HERE, ON WINDY ISLAND!
THAT BUSYBODY HAS DISCOVERED MY SECRET!
I UNDER-ESTIMATED HER... AND THEY'RE RUINING EVERY-THING!
I SPENT A FORTUNE BUILDING MY COLLECTION! I WENT AGAINST EVERY INTERNATIONAL LAW TO CAPTURE PROTECTED SPECIES...
...AND NOW MY DREAM IS BEING BLOWN TO BITS!

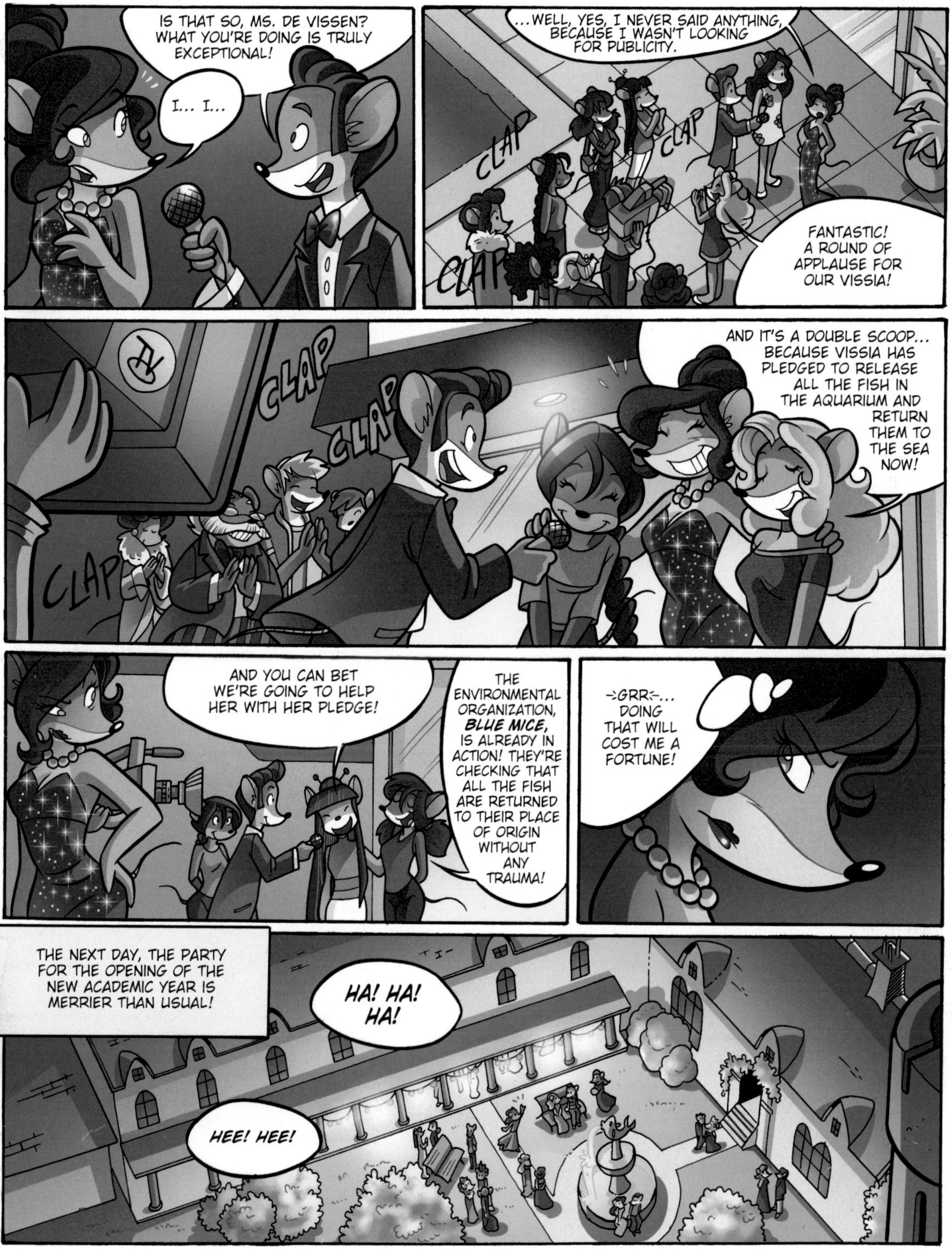
IS THAT SO, MS. DE VISSEN? WHAT YOU'RE DOING IS TRULY EXCEPTIONAL!
I... I...
...WELL, YES, I NEVER SAID ANYTHING, BECAUSE I WASN'T LOOKING FOR PUBLICITY.
CLAP CLAP CLAP
FANTASTIC! A ROUND OF APPLAUSE FOR OUR VISSIA!
CLAP CLAP CLAP
AND IT'S A DOUBLE SCOOP... BECAUSE VISSIA HAS PLEDGED TO RELEASE ALL THE FISH IN THE AQUARIUM AND RETURN THEM TO THE SEA NOW!
AND YOU CAN BET WE'RE GOING TO HELP HER WITH HER PLEDGE!
THE ENVIRONMENTAL ORGANIZATION, BLUE MICE, IS ALREADY IN ACTION! THEY'RE CHECKING THAT ALL THE FISH ARE RETURNED TO THEIR PLACE OF ORIGIN WITHOUT ANY TRAUMA!
GRR... DOING THAT WILL COST ME A FORTUNE!
THE NEXT DAY, THE PARTY FOR THE OPENING OF THE NEW ACADEMIC YEAR IS MERRIER THAN USUAL!
HA! HA! HA!
HEE! HEE!

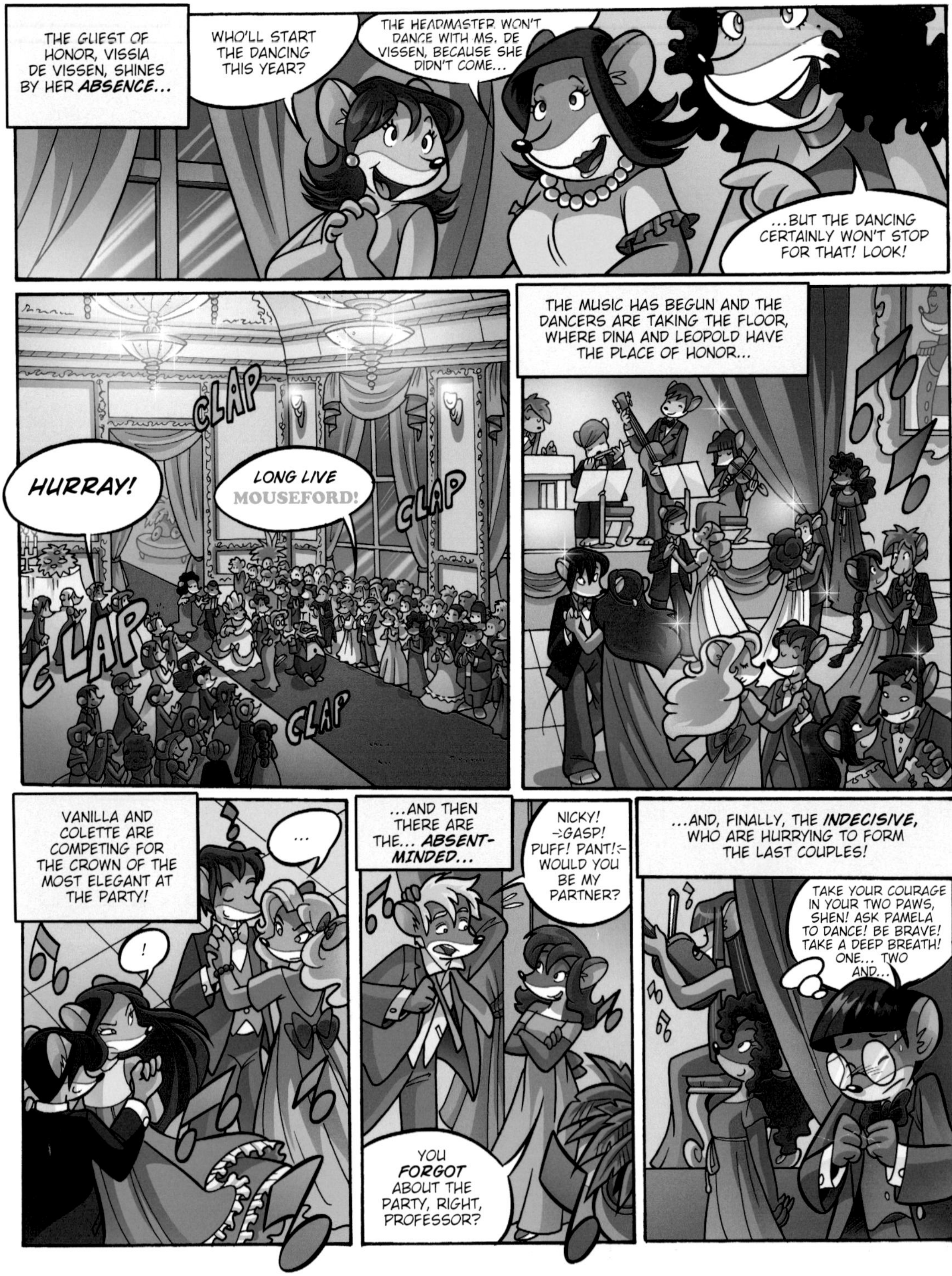

THE GUEST OF HONOR, VISSIA DE VISSEN, SHINES BY HER ABSENCE...
WHO'LL START THE DANCING THIS YEAR?
THE HEADMASTER WON'T DANCE WITH MS. DE VISSEN, BECAUSE SHE DIDN'T COME...
...BUT THE DANCING CERTAINLY WON'T STOP FOR THAT! LOOK!
CLAP
HURRAY!
LONG LIVE MOUSEFORD!
CLAP
CLAP
CLAP
THE MUSIC HAS BEGUN AND THE DANCERS ARE TAKING THE FLOOR, WHERE DINA AND LEOPOLD HAVE THE PLACE OF HONOR...
VANILLA AND COLETTE ARE COMPETING FOR THE CROWN OF THE MOST ELEGANT AT THE PARTY!
...
!
...AND THEN THERE ARE THE... ABSENT-MINDED...
NICKY! →GASP! PUFF! PANT!← WOULD YOU BE MY PARTNER?
YOU FORGOT ABOUT THE PARTY, RIGHT, PROFESSOR?
...AND, FINALLY, THE INDECISIVE, WHO ARE HURRYING TO FORM THE LAST COUPLES!
TAKE YOUR COURAGE IN YOUR TWO PAWS, SHEN! ASK PAMELA TO DANCE! BE BRAVE! TAKE A DEEP BREATH! ONE... TWO AND...

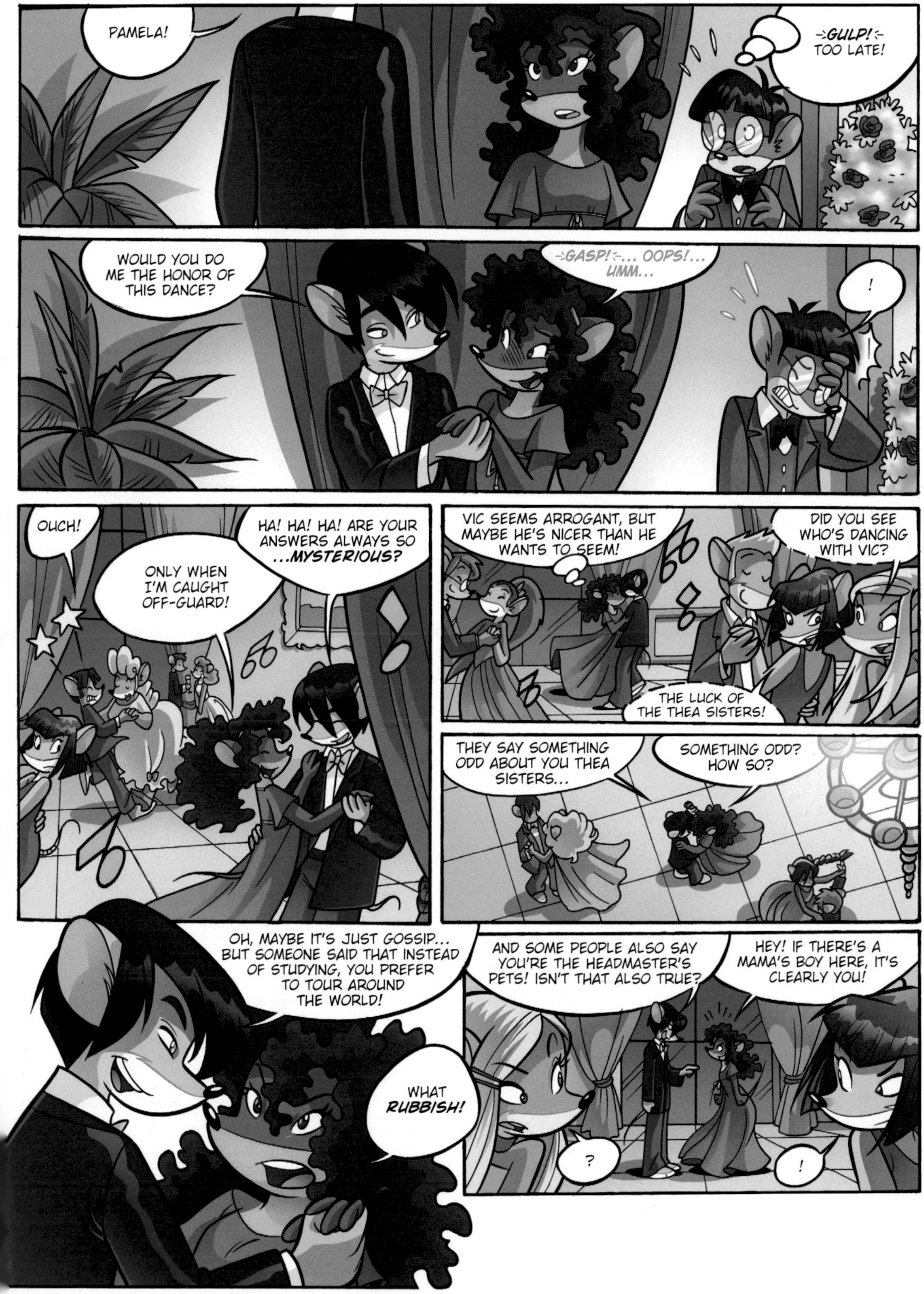
PAMELA!
GULP! TOO LATE!
WOULD YOU DO ME THE HONOR OF THIS DANCE?
GASP!... OOPS!... UMM...
!
OUCH!
HA! HA! HA! ARE YOUR ANSWERS ALWAYS SO ...MYSTERIOUS?
ONLY WHEN I'M CAUGHT OFF-GUARD!
VIC SEEMS ARROGANT, BUT MAYBE HE'S NICER THAN HE WANTS TO SEEM!
DID YOU SEE WHO'S DANCING WITH VIC?
THE LUCK OF THE THEA SISTERS!
THEY SAY SOMETHING ODD ABOUT YOU THEA SISTERS...
SOMETHING ODD? HOW SO?
OH, MAYBE IT'S JUST GOSSIP... BUT SOMEONE SAID THAT INSTEAD OF STUDYING, YOU PREFER TO TOUR AROUND THE WORLD!
WHAT RUBBISH!
AND SOME PEOPLE ALSO SAY YOU'RE THE HEADMASTER'S PETS! ISN'T THAT ALSO TRUE?
HEY! IF THERE'S A MAMA'S BOY HERE, IT'S CLEARLY YOU!
?
!

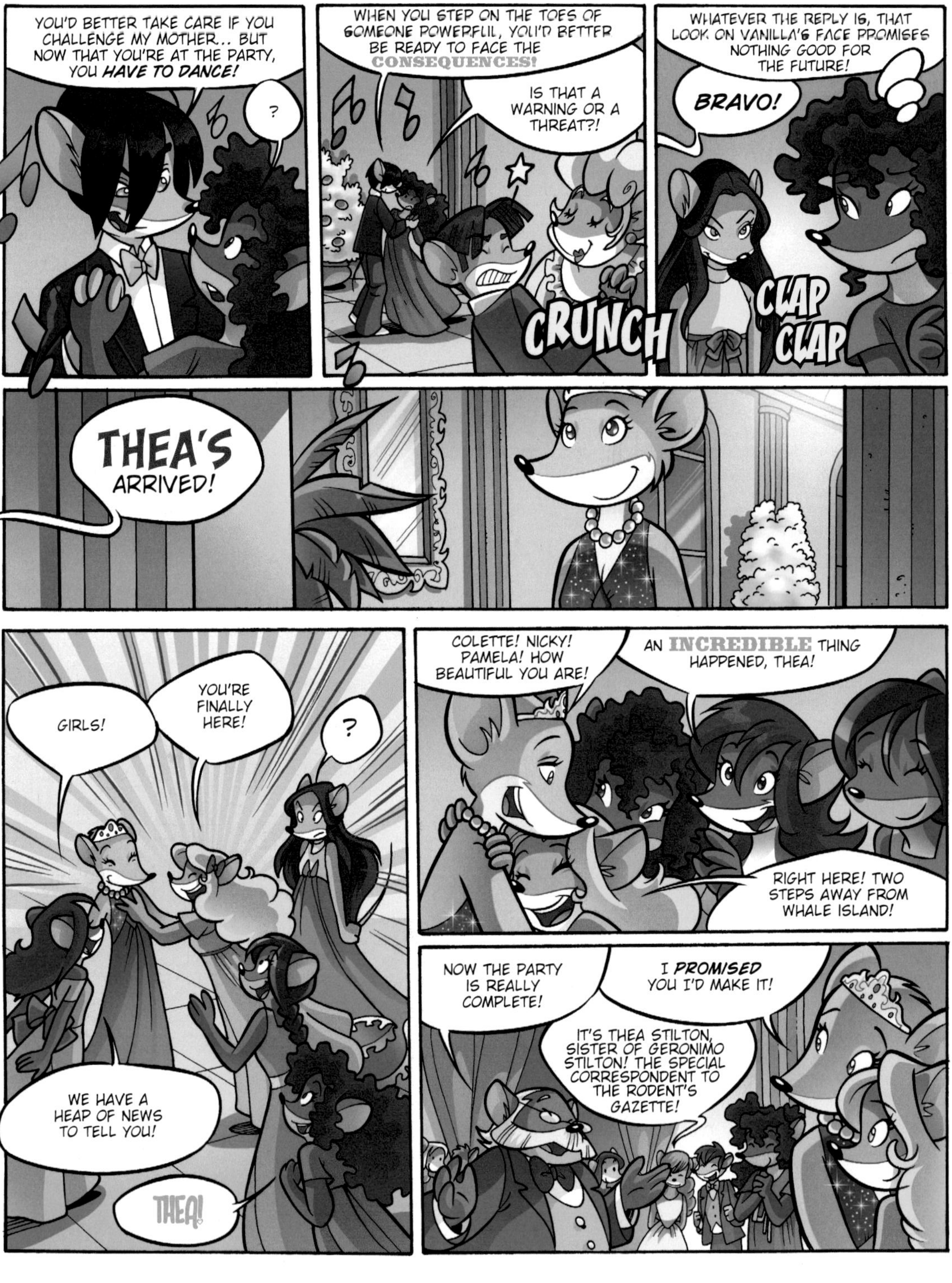
YOU'D BETTER TAKE CARE IF YOU CHALLENGE MY MOTHER... BUT NOW THAT YOU'RE AT THE PARTY, YOU HAVE TO DANCE!
?
WHEN YOU STEP ON THE TOES OF SOMEONE POWERFUL, YOU'D BETTER BE READY TO FACE THE CONSEQUENCES!
IS THAT A WARNING OR A THREAT?!
CRUNCH
WHATEVER THE REPLY IS, THAT LOOK ON VANILLA'S FACE PROMISES NOTHING GOOD FOR THE FUTURE!
BRAVO!
CLAP CLAP
THEA'S ARRIVED!
GIRLS!
YOU'RE FINALLY HERE!
?
WE HAVE A HEAP OF NEWS TO TELL YOU!
THEA!
COLETTE! NICKY! PAMELA! HOW BEAUTIFUL YOU ARE!
AN INCREDIBLE THING HAPPENED, THEA!
RIGHT HERE! TWO STEPS AWAY FROM WHALE ISLAND!
NOW THE PARTY IS REALLY COMPLETE!
I PROMISED YOU I'D MAKE IT!
IT'S THEA STILTON, SISTER OF GERONIMO STILTON! THE SPECIAL CORRESPONDENT TO THE RODENT'S GAZETTE!

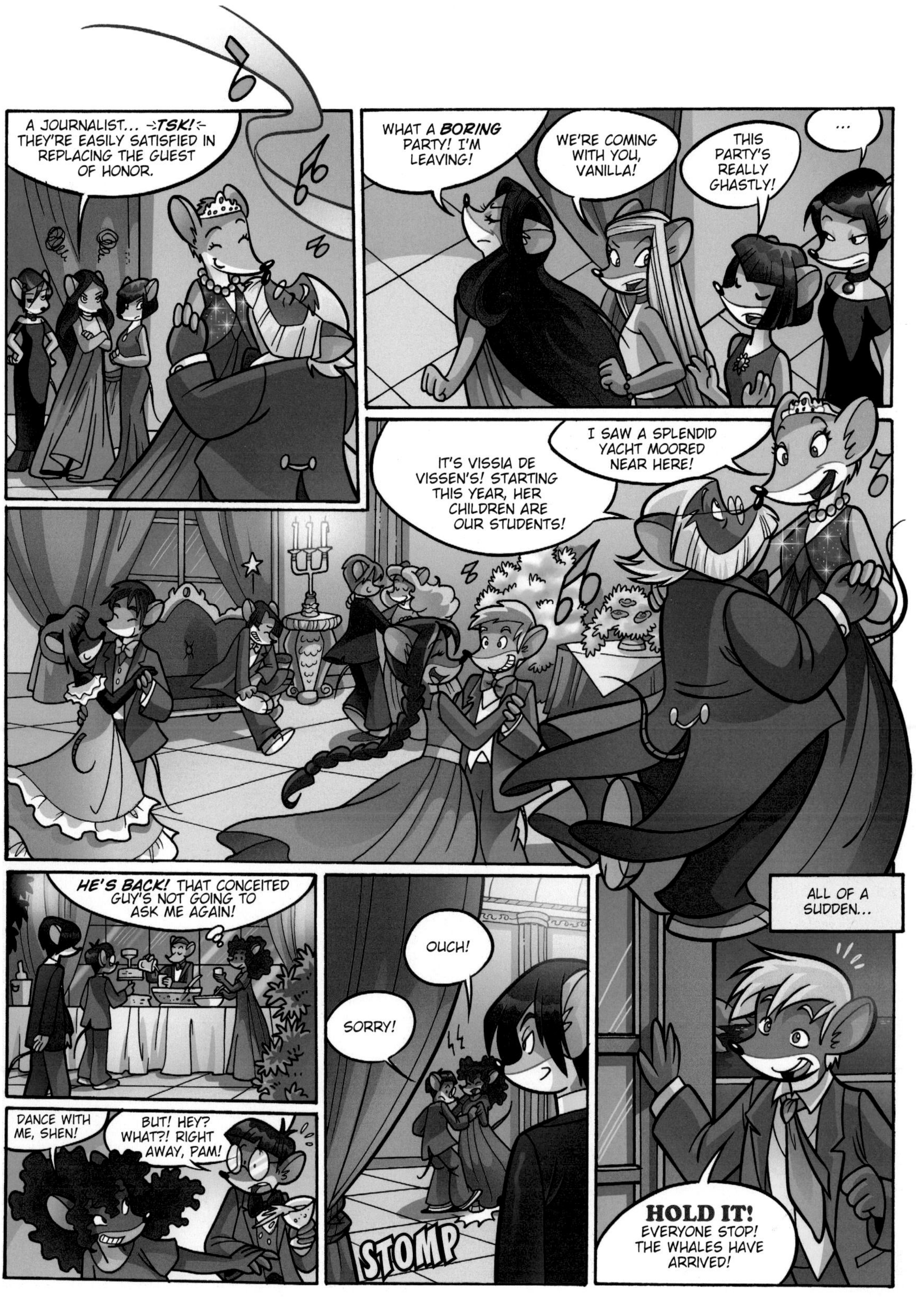
A JOURNALIST... TSK! THEY'RE EASILY SATISFIED IN REPLACING THE GUEST OF HONOR.
WHAT A BORING PARTY! I'M LEAVING!
WE'RE COMING WITH YOU, VANILLA!
THIS PARTY'S REALLY GHASTLY!
...
I SAW A SPLENDID YACHT MOORED NEAR HERE!
IT'S VISSIA DE VISSEN'S! STARTING THIS YEAR, HER CHILDREN ARE OUR STUDENTS!
HE'S BACK! THAT CONCEITED GUY'S NOT GOING TO ASK ME AGAIN!
DANCE WITH ME, SHEN!
BUT! HEY? WHAT?! RIGHT AWAY, PAM!
OUCH!
SORRY!
STOMP
ALL OF A SUDDEN...
HOLD IT! EVERYONE STOP! THE WHALES HAVE ARRIVED!

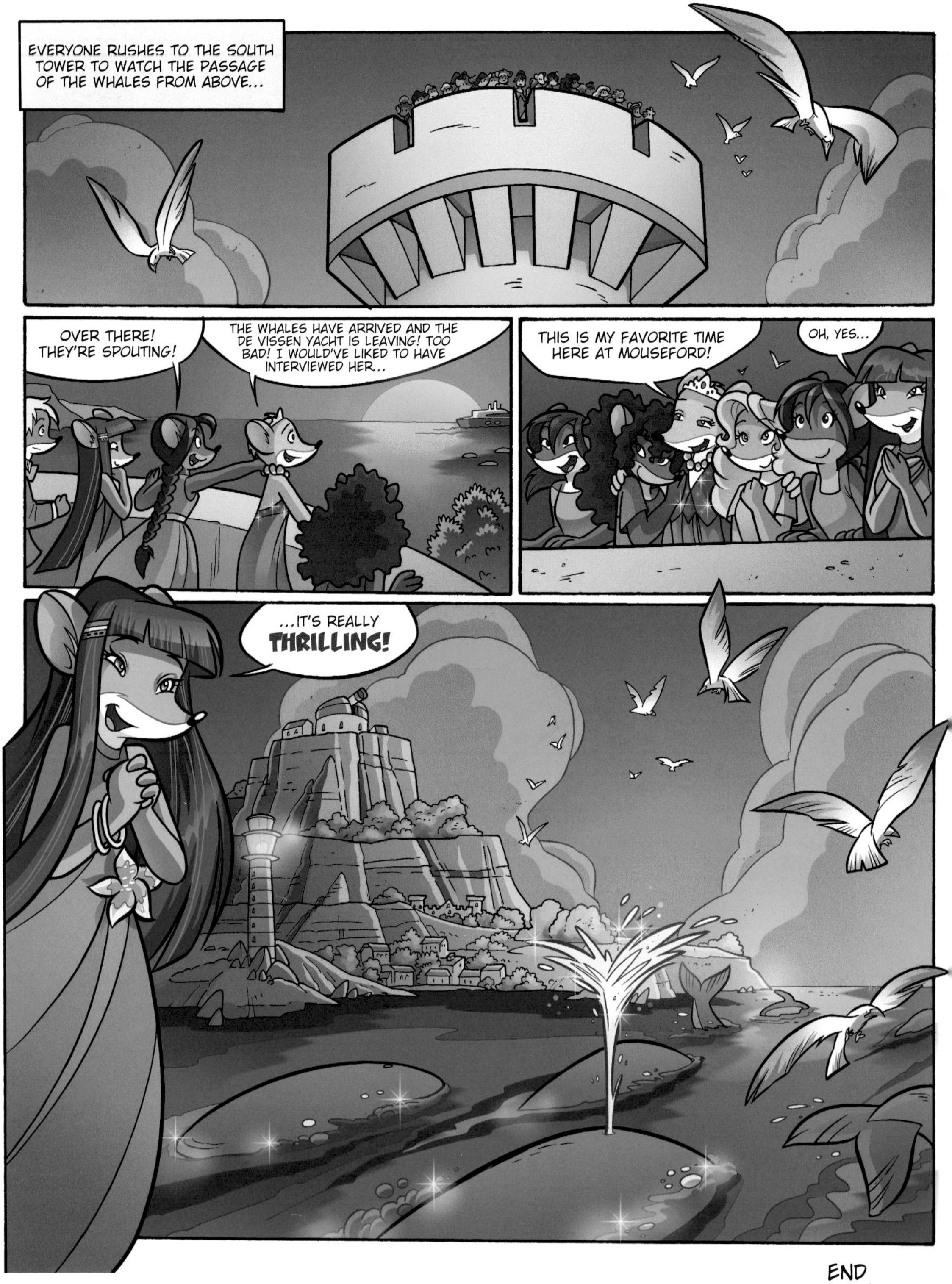
EVERYONE RUSHES TO THE SOUTH TOWER TO WATCH THE PASSAGE OF THE WHALES FROM ABOVE...
OVER THERE! THEY'RE SPOUTING!
THE WHALES HAVE ARRIVED AND THE DE VISSEN YACHT IS LEAVING! TOO BAD! I WOULD'VE LIKED TO HAVE INTERVIEWED HER...
THIS IS MY FAVORITE TIME HERE AT MOUSEFORD!
OH, YES...
...IT'S REALLY THRILLING!
END

Watch Out For PAPERCUTZ™

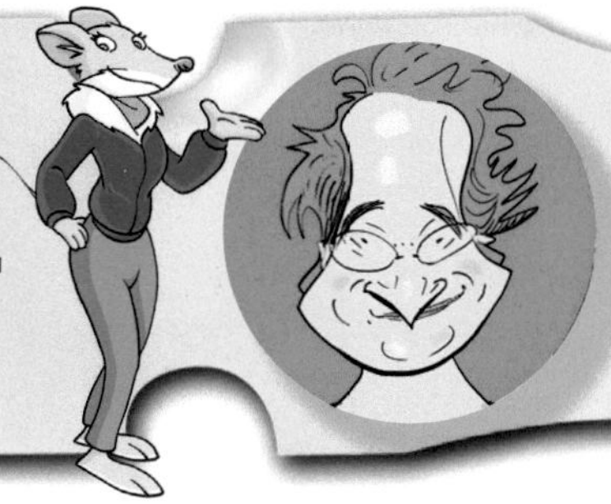

Welcome to Whale Island! Er, no, no I meant, welcome to Freshman Orientation at Mouseford Academy! Wait, that's not it, either! Oh, I remember now… welcome to the premiere THEA STILTON graphic novel from Papercutz, the furry folks dedicated to publishing great graphic novels for all ages! I'm Salicrup, *Jim Salicrup*, the Editor-in-Chief of the Rodent's Gazette. Oops! That's not right either! Geronimo Stilton is the Editor-in-Chief of the Rodent's Gazette! I'm the Editor-in-Chief of Papercutz!

I apologize for all the confusion, but things have been a little crazy around here lately. Ever since we announced that we would also be publishing THEA STILTON graphic novels, Thea's many fans have been eagerly awaiting her solo-graphic novel debut. But, you see, that's where the confusion comes in! Thea's fans, after watching her in action with her brother Geronimo Stilton in his graphic novel series, naturally assumed that a new graphic novel series entitled THEA STILTON would star the world-famouse Special Correspondent for the Rodent's Gazette in her very own adventures. Well, while Thea does appear in THEA STILTON, the real stars are the Thea Sisters. And no, they're not Thea's sisters, either! They're five students at Mouseford Academy who want to become real live journalists, just like their idol, Thea Stilton! So, with Thea's blessing and support, Colette, Violet, Pamela, Nicky, and Paulina have formed a sorority called "The Thea Sisters," named after you-know-who!

-Whew!- Now that we we've cleared all that up (I hope), let's take a sneak peek, on the following pages, at what's coming up in GERONIMO STILTON #13 "The Fastest Train in the West," which will soon be coming down the tracks! And don't forget to look out for THEA STILTON #2 "The Revenge of the Lizard Club," also slithering its way to you soon! And if that's not enough Stilton family fun for you, don't forget to visit www.geronimostilton.com for even more fun!

Class dismissed!

Jim

Stay in Touch!

EMAIL:	salicrup@papercutz.com
WEB:	www.papercutz.com
TWITTER:	@papercutzgn
FACEBOOK:	PAPERCUTZGRAPHICNOVELS
FAN MAIL:	Papercutz, 160 Broadway, Suite 700, East Wing, New York, NY 10038

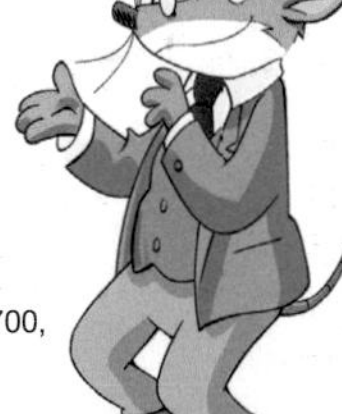

Caricature of Jim by Steve Brodner at the MoCCA Art Fest.

Geronimo Stilton boxed sets!
Three Graphic Novels
collected in each box!

©Atlantyca S.p.A.

Available at booksellers everywhere.

Special Preview of GERONIMO STILTON #13 "The Fastest Train in the West"!

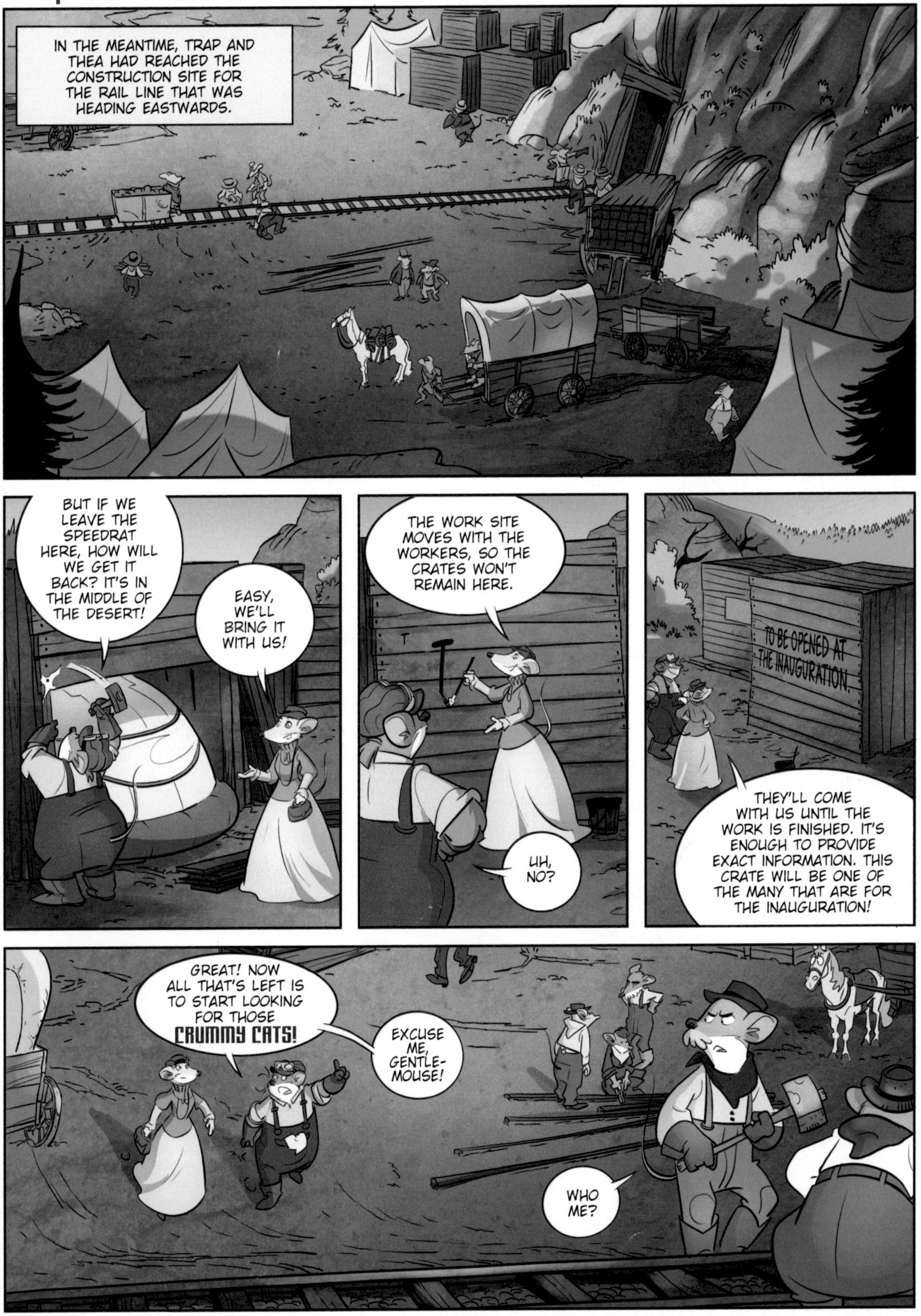
IN THE MEANTIME, TRAP AND THEA HAD REACHED THE CONSTRUCTION SITE FOR THE RAIL LINE THAT WAS HEADING EASTWARDS.
BUT IF WE LEAVE THE SPEEDRAT HERE, HOW WILL WE GET IT BACK? IT'S IN THE MIDDLE OF THE DESERT!
EASY, WE'LL BRING IT WITH US!
THE WORK SITE MOVES WITH THE WORKERS, SO THE CRATES WON'T REMAIN HERE.
UH, NO?
TO BE OPENED AT THE INAUGURATION.
THEY'LL COME WITH US UNTIL THE WORK IS FINISHED. IT'S ENOUGH TO PROVIDE EXACT INFORMATION. THIS CRATE WILL BE ONE OF THE MANY THAT ARE FOR THE INAUGURATION!
GREAT! NOW ALL THAT'S LEFT IS TO START LOOKING FOR THOSE CRUMMY CATS!
EXCUSE ME, GENTLE-MOUSE!
WHO ME?

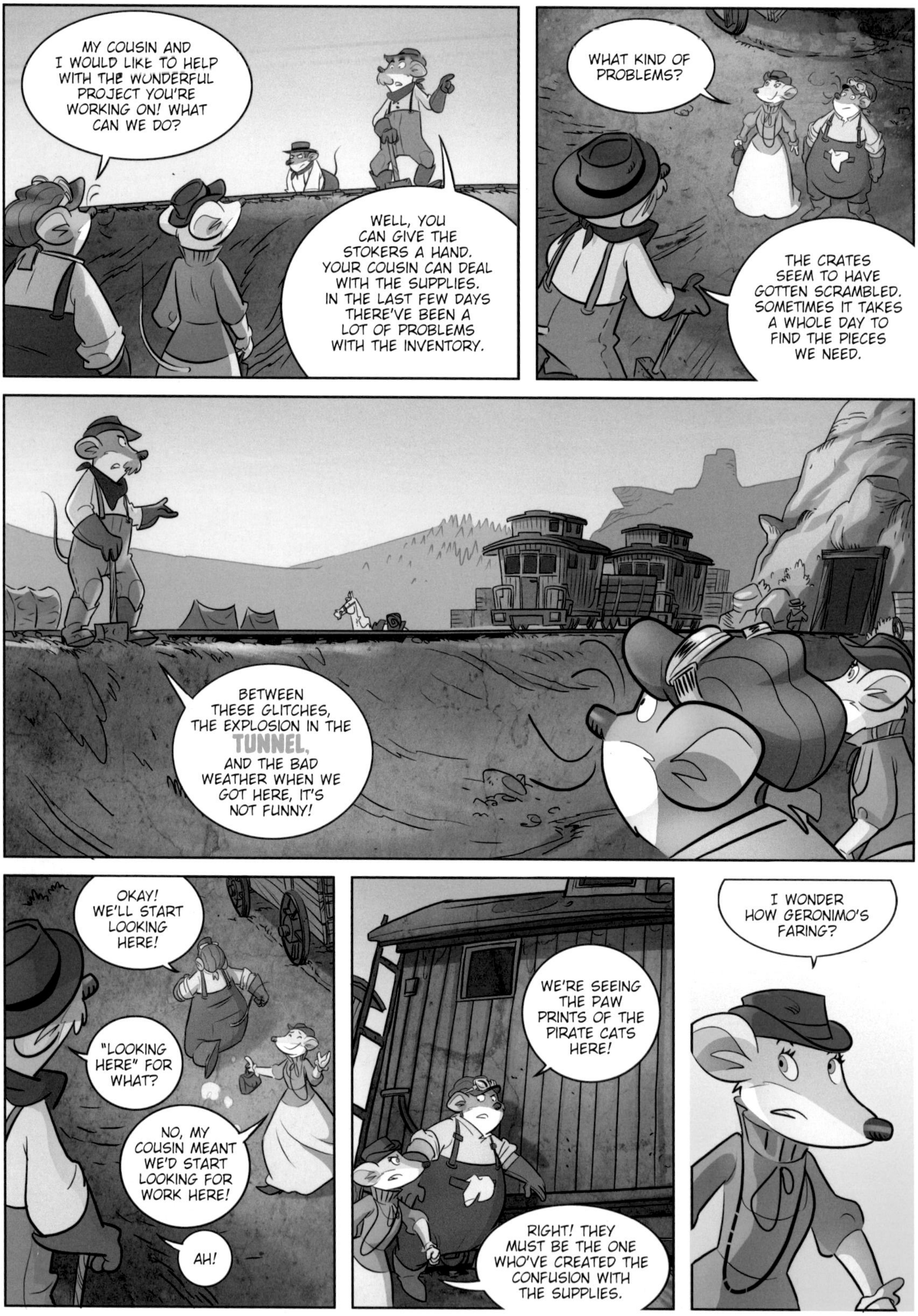
MY COUSIN AND I WOULD LIKE TO HELP WITH THE WONDERFUL PROJECT YOU'RE WORKING ON! WHAT CAN WE DO?
WELL, YOU CAN GIVE THE STOKERS A HAND. YOUR COUSIN CAN DEAL WITH THE SUPPLIES. IN THE LAST FEW DAYS THERE'VE BEEN A LOT OF PROBLEMS WITH THE INVENTORY.
WHAT KIND OF PROBLEMS?
THE CRATES SEEM TO HAVE GOTTEN SCRAMBLED. SOMETIMES IT TAKES A WHOLE DAY TO FIND THE PIECES WE NEED.
BETWEEN THESE GLITCHES, THE EXPLOSION IN THE TUNNEL, AND THE BAD WEATHER WHEN WE GOT HERE, IT'S NOT FUNNY!
OKAY! WE'LL START LOOKING HERE!
"LOOKING HERE" FOR WHAT?
NO, MY COUSIN MEANT WE'D START LOOKING FOR WORK HERE!
AH!
WE'RE SEEING THE PAW PRINTS OF THE PIRATE CATS HERE!
RIGHT! THEY MUST BE THE ONE WHO'VE CREATED THE CONFUSION WITH THE SUPPLIES.
I WONDER HOW GERONIMO'S FARING?

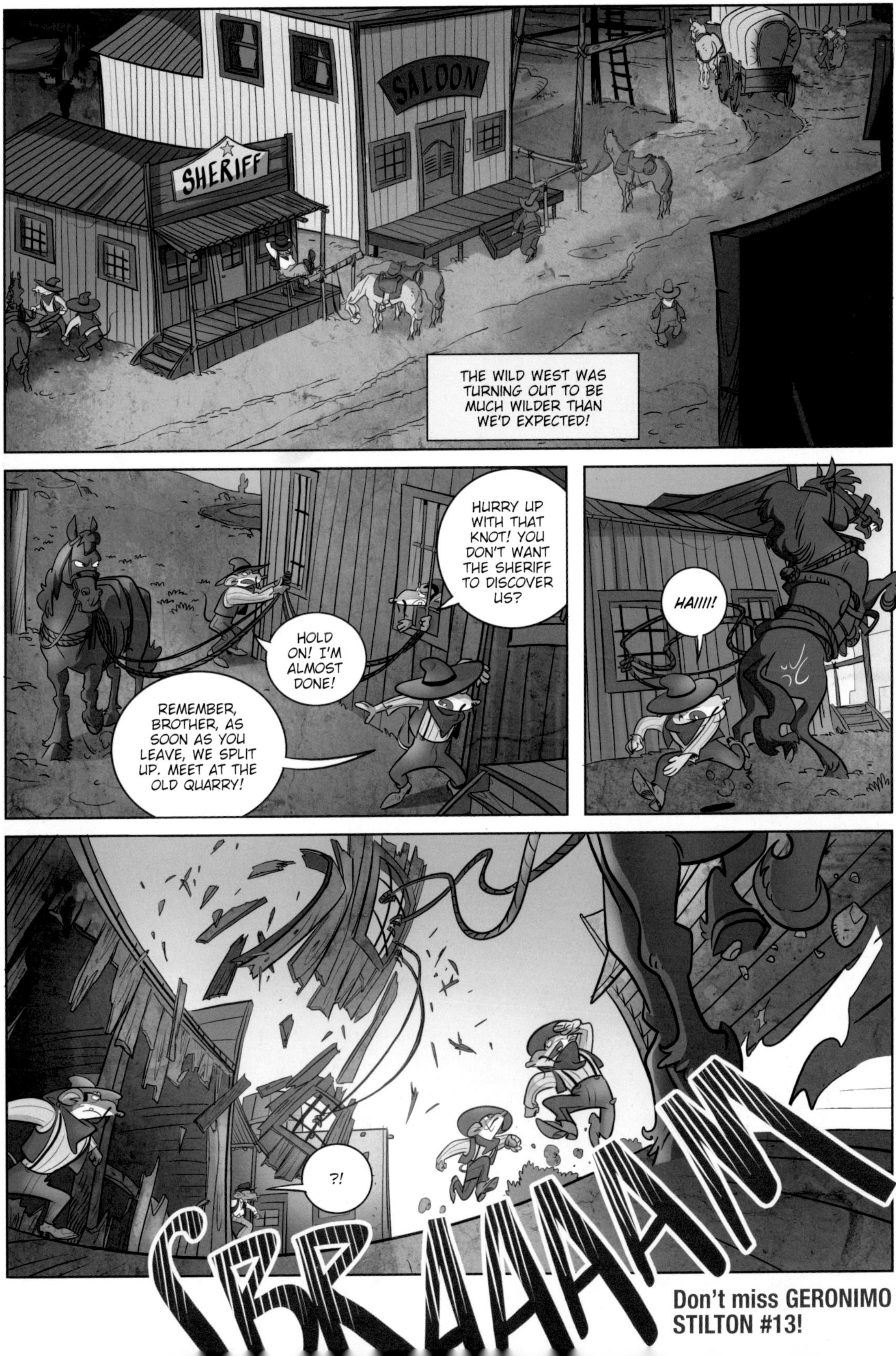

SHERIFF
SALOON
THE WILD WEST WAS TURNING OUT TO BE MUCH WILDER THAN WE'D EXPECTED!
HURRY UP WITH THAT KNOT! YOU DON'T WANT THE SHERIFF TO DISCOVER US?
HOLD ON! I'M ALMOST DONE!
REMEMBER, BROTHER, AS SOON AS YOU LEAVE, WE SPLIT UP. MEET AT THE OLD QUARRY!
HAIII!!
?!

Don't miss GERONIMO STILTON #13!

More Great Graphic Novels from PAPERCUTZ

NEW STORIES! FULL-COLOR GRAPHIC NOVEL
Disney FAIRIES
Tinker Bell and the Most Precious Gift
PAPERCUTZ

DISNEY FAIRIES #11

"Tinker Bell and the Most Precious Gift"

Four magical tales featuring the fairies from Pixie Hollow!

Guillaume Bianco
Antonello Dalena
Ernest & Rebecca

ERNEST & REBECCA #4

"The Land of Walking Stones"

A 6 ½ year old girl and her microbial buddy against the world!

GARFIELD
SECRET AGENT X
PAPERCUTZ

GARFIELD & Co #8

"Secret Agent X"

As seen on the Cartoon Network!

Monster Turkey
PAPERCUTZ

MONSTER #4

"Monster Turkey"

The almost normal adventures of an almost ordinary family... with a pet monster!

SMURFS
THE BABY SMURF
PAPERCUTZ

THE SMURFS #14

"The Baby Smurf"

There's a new arrival in the Smurfs Village!

SYBIL
the Backpack Fairy
"AITHOR"
Rodrigue
Dalena
Razzi
PAPERCUTZ

SYBIL THE BACKPACK FAIRY #3

"Aithor"

What's cooler than a fairy in your backpack? How about a flying horse?!

Available at better booksellers everywhere!

Or order directly from us! DISNEY FAIRIES is available in paperback for $7.99, in hardcover for $11.99; ERNEST & REBECCA is $11.99 in hardcover only; GARFIELD & Co is available in hardcover only for $7.99; MONSTER is available in hardcover only for $9.99; THE SMURFS are available in paperback for $5.99, in hardcover for $10.99; and SYBIL THE BACKPACK FAIRY is available in hardcover only for $11.99.

Please add $4.00 for postage and handling for the first book, add $1.00 for each additional book.
Please make check payable to NBM Publishing Send to: PAPERCUTZ,160 Broadway, Suite 700, East Wing, New York, NY 10038
(1-800-886-1223)

WHERE THE ANCIENT AND PRESTIGIOUS **MOUSEFORD ACADEMY** CAN BE FOUND!

YOU DON'T WANT TO BE OUR GUEST, MADAM? I CAN RESERVE A ROOM AT THE INN FOR YOU!

PLEASE DON'T BOTHER! I PREFER THE *SUITE* ONBOARD MY YACHT!

SLEEP IN A COUNTRY INN! HOW **AWFUL!**

BESIDES... I HAVE MORE IMPORTANT THINGS TO DO!

Vissia de Vissen is the queen of cosmetics. She's rich and famous, but she's also greedy and unscrupulous! Colette thinks she's really first rate, but is she actually?

Vic de Vissen is Vissia's son and also a new student at Mouseford Academy... Will it be love between Vic and Pamela?

WOULD YOU DO ME THE HONOR OF THIS DANCE?

~GASP!~... OOPS!... UMM...

!